REBEL

HELLION MC #1

AVA MANELLO

Nikki
Thanks for helping
to bring our girl to
life Love
Ava Manello x

Rebel by Ava Manello

© 2018, Ava Manello

KBK Publishing

ISBN: 978-0-9932436-3-9

Cover Designer: Francessca Wingfield

I thought long and hard about who I should dedicate this book to, in the end there was only one person. Without my amazing cover designer, Francessca Wingfield, asking me what I thought of a cover she had designed, this book would never have existed. I fell in love with the cover at first sight, and within minutes had conjured up Rebel and her dads'. The cover inspired the whole book. So this book is for you Fran, to celebrate your amazing covers and to thank you for the friendship, support and encouragement over the years.

Rebel will always be 'Our Girl' and I hope that you enjoy her story as much as I enjoyed writing it.

PROLOGUE

Jackson

I pull my bike off the highway, ready to turn into the clubhouse gates. I'm pissed to notice a cardboard box dumped in front of them and blocking my path. Lowering the Harley onto its kickstand I dismount, I'll have to move the bloody thing before I can open the gate.

The box lid is loosely folded over on itself and I almost drop it when I hear a mewling sound coming from inside, for fucks sake, I hope no one's been stupid enough to dump a puppy on us. Do we really look like the local animal shelter?

I'm shocked to shit when I discover that it's not a puppy in the box, it's a baby. Inquisitive blue eyes stare up at me and a tiny fist reaches up as if to touch me. I make a harrumph kind of noise in my throat and am rewarded with a gurgle in response. I'd say it was accompanied by a smile, but I'm pretty sure I remember my sister telling me that my nephew was too young to smile when he was that small, it's just wind. I don't know about that, must've just been coincidence that he had wind every time I picked him up.

I turn my attention back to the infant in front of me. Why the hell would anyone dump a baby, especially outside a clubhouse full of bikers? A convent I could understand, a children's home even, but a clubhouse? I don't think any of us have any idea how to deal with this.

Gently, taking care not to jostle the little one, I cradle it in my arms. I'm rewarded with coos and giggles and an appalling aroma of soiled diaper. Man, I need to find someone to hand this situation over to. I can't even tell if it's a boy or a girl from the anonymous white baby grow they're dressed in.

I press the intercom, calling for help to come to the gates. Bill doesn't believe me at first when I tell him why I need help, reluctantly agreeing to come and assist. Looking down in the box I spot an envelope. I'll have to wait for Bill to get here before I can read it, I don't think I can juggle the baby and the letter. The tiny infant seems remarkably content snuggled in between my leather cut and my arm. I touch my finger gently against its nose and am rewarded with a small fist grasping tightly to my finger.

Bill makes his way to the gate far too slowly for my liking, he's dawdling along like he's on an afternoon stroll for fucks sake. I swear at him to hurry up, then realize I need to watch my language in front of the child. Bikers and babies are not a good mix.

I'm rewarded by a suitable look of shock on his face when he realizes I was telling the truth.

"What the fuck?" he exclaims.

"Watch your mouth." I warn, gesturing with my head to the infant in my arms.

Bill reaches for the baby, but surprisingly, I'm reluctant to let go. Instead, I tell him about the envelope. He takes it from the box, opens it and starts reading it out loud.

Hellion M.C

The property in this box belongs to you. She's the unwanted outcome of a night of partying with you guys last year. I think it's only fair you take responsibility as none of you saw fit to use protection. I'm afraid I don't know which of you is the father, could be any one of you. She's the result of my one night of rebellion, and I won't pay the price of that for the rest of my life. She's your problem now.

The note isn't signed. I can't believe anyone would dump a baby so casually. I'm enraged at the heartlessness the mother has shown and the cowardly way out she's chosen. I look at the little girl in my arms, the smile is back on her face, and wind or not, that's the moment I realize this tiny soul has stolen my heart already.

CHAPTER ONE

Thirty years later

Rebel

I close the door of my office on the main street; stretching my shoulders out after a long day spent pouring over my MacBook screen analyzing figures. I love my job and being my own boss, but sometimes I just need to kick back and forget all about it. That's what tonight is all about. It's my thirtieth birthday, and my Dads' are throwing me a party at the clubhouse. I feel a little guilty as I haven't been to see them for a few weeks. Work has been so busy thanks to tourist season and the local hotels and guest houses passing their accounts my way, that I feel like I've neglected them.

I loosen the collar of my formal blouse and inhale a large

gulp of fresh air. I love the outdoors. It's why I chose to set up my practice here rather than in Victoria. The built-up city would have stifled me. Maldon is one of the original gold rush towns and still has some amazing nineteenth century properties that attract a healthy tourist trade. It's a small town really, at best we have a population of 1500 or so, and it's one of those places where everyone knows your business. It was hard growing up knowing that any mischief I got into would be reported to my Dads' before I made it back to the Clubhouse, yet it was a safe and loving environment as well. I couldn't have asked for a better childhood.

Moving to Victoria to take my Bachelor of Business degree was hard, but at least I was close enough to have regular visits home. It was worth it as it meant I qualified as an Accountant and was able to set up a small but successful practice here in Maldon. I smile as several clients shout birthday greetings to me while I make my way past their stores on the shaded main street. Whilst Maldon often has more tourists than locals, this is one of those quieter spells in between the festivals and fairs, where the hotels aren't packed to capacity. It's one of my favorite times of year.

The drive back to my cottage in Castlemaine takes just over fifteen minutes, still it's long enough to enjoy the chill of the air con. I haven't lived at the Clubhouse since I left for University, much to my Dads' dismay. They didn't want me to leave, but I needed to be my own person. I guess I've lived up to my name, Rebel; it's short for Rebellion. Apparently, I was a bit of a handful as a baby, and they named me accordingly.

Because I was abandoned, they'd had a few months of arguing with the local authorities about keeping custody of me and registering my birth. Time enough to see my personality and for the nickname they'd given me to stick. Although tonight's the night we celebrate my birthday, it's more the anniversary of the day they found me, abandoned outside the Clubhouse by my callous mother. No one knows my true date of birth. I should be bitter about being abandoned, the state called me a Foundling, but I can't be. I couldn't have asked for more love, understanding and care than I have had from my Dads' these last thirty years.

You maybe think it odd that I call them my Dads', plural, but we've never done the DNA test to find out which of them is my biological father. They never felt the need, and once I was old enough to understand, I didn't want to either.

Shutting the door of my cottage behind me, I take pleasure in kicking off my heels as I head for my walk-in shower. The strong pulsing of the warm water on my shoulders and neck revives me. I let my head drop down, enjoying the sensation and following the rivulets of water as they cascade over my tattoos. I have a full chest piece with wings, a heart and 'true love forever' to represent my Dads', whilst my arms are a trellis of flowers and leaves. I cover them while I'm at work, although I don't really need to. The majority of my clients know I have them and accept them, just as they accept me. It's something a rather pushy university professor gave me a lot of grief over and it stuck with me.

I step out of the shower, wrapped in a large, soft towel and head to my wardrobe. I've bought a simple strapless black dress for tonight and I'm pairing it with my five-inch black heels. I'll put my hair up, with a few loose curling tendrils. Jackson likes to see me look 'classy' as he calls it. I know I shouldn't have a favorite Dad, but he's always been the one I've felt closest to. He's the one who found me, then fought to keep me; although the rest of the Club gave him their unfailing support. He's also the one that encouraged my love of Accountancy, he's the Club Treasurer and from an early age I'd sit and watch him whilst he did the books. When I started showing an interest, he'd take time out to explain it all to me.

Hellion MC may be the club name, but I'm the rowdiest and most mischievous member of the Club; the only one that lives up to the title. The guys are mostly retired ex-military, and nothing like the MC's you see on TV or in the movies. They don't deal in guns, although they do run a gun club. They don't deal in drugs, but a couple of them run a garden center. They're good guys, who are model citizens. They just have a few tattoos and beards and ride bikes. It doesn't make them bad people, and I hate the stereotypes and assumptions some of the tourists make when they see them. Once you get to know them you soon realize, they're nothing more than giant, gentle teddy bears. Just don't let them know I called them that!

I apply some smoky eye shadow, a nude lipstick and

contour my cheeks. I look nothing like the professional business owner from earlier in the day. My reflection in the mirror shows a girl ready to party, and that's exactly what I am.

I throw my overnight bag into the car and head for the Clubhouse, it's only a short ride away in Nuggety. I decided against taking my bike as this dress may be hot, but it's totally unsuitable. I can't wait to see my Dads' again and celebrate this special day with them.

CHAPTER TWO

Rebel

I park my Kia Sportage at the side of the clubhouse and take a moment to enjoy the feeling of coming home. I love my little brick and timber cottage, and the history that goes with it, but this place with all its steel and modernity will always hold my heart. This is where I was raised and where my Dads' are.

The clubhouse is set in a lot of acreage and there's nothing around for miles. Because many of the guys in the MC are ex-veterans, they relished the peace and quiet here when they came home from duty. I have to laugh when I watch shows on TV that portray MC's as drug and gun running bad guys. It's as far from the life I grew up in as possible.

Granted back in the day, when I first appeared, they were womanizers, but they've aged a lot since then and become settled. Many of them have old ladies and kids, and the average age is around sixty now. The club needs some new blood, but they're not interested in young hot heads as Jackson calls them. I'm one of the odd ones as most of their kids have moved away to the city, life around here is too quiet for them I guess, but that's what I love most.

The dull thud of music from inside the building draws me in, music has always been a big part of my life and I love that my Dads' allowed me the freedom to make my own choices when it comes to music, although I'm probably massively influenced by the stuff they played when I was growing up. I like a lot of American indie rock like Hinder and Shinedown, and the odd Five Finger Death Punch if I'm in the mood, but I'll always have a soft spot for Elvis, Johnny Cash and the like. Hearing those songs from my childhood always brings back memories of laughter and being surrounded by love.

The front door of the clubhouse opens, pulling me from my memories. It's Jackson and I let out a whoop as I run up to him and he pulls me into that encompassing bear hug of his. He smells of soap and leather, a combination I love.

"Happy birthday, darlin'," he whispers in my ear.

"Thanks, old man." I chuckle, taking in yet more grey highlights in his once dark hair. He's turning into a silver fox, and if anything is even better looking than he was as a young man.

"Less of the old," he admonishes, "you're not too big to go over my knee and get a spanking you disrespectful girl." He's grinning as he tells me off, although I suspect if the occasion warranted it, he wouldn't spare me when it comes to discipline. My Dads' have always been firm but fair in that respect.

He finally relinquishes his hold and steps back to assess me. The look of approval on his face means everything to me. "Wow, you scrub up well," he shakes his head almost to himself. "You're definitely going to break some hearts my girl." Taking hold of my hand he opens the door and pulls me into the party behind him. "Hey everyone, our girl's arrived!"

The party is in full swing when I enter, and I see so many familiar faces it warms my heart. Looks like a lot of my cousins and their families have joined us from out of town to celebrate my special day. Whilst they've moved away there's always something happening to bring them back be it family barbecues, special birthdays or Christmas. I've always felt sorry for those with normal families, how boring it must be only celebrating with a few people, when I get to celebrate with this huge extended family of mine.

"Rebel!" A blonde rushes towards me, almost knocking me over in her haste to greet me. I can't help laughing at her. Chastity is my best friend, and you'd think she hadn't seen me in forever, despite the fact she was only at my house last night for pizza and a movie. She's a bit ditzy on occasion but I love her to bits, we go way back, although she's an outsider. Her family moved to Maldon the first year of high school and we've been inseparable ever since, even rooming together at Uni.

Chastity wraps her arms around me so tightly I think she's

going to snap me in half. Laughing I push her away. "How much have you had to drink girl?" She has that glint in her eyes that tells me she's had enough to let loose, but not that much she's drunk yet. She's left her dark blonde hair hanging straight behind her shoulders, wearing just enough make up to enhance her dark brown eyes, but she's gone for a natural palette. She'd look like the girl next door if it wasn't for her nose ring, too afraid to get a tattoo it was her teenage rebellion against her parents. I love this girl like a sister, and I know the feeling is mutual. Our friendship hasn't been easy, her overly religious parents weren't keen on her befriending the little girl born of sin who was being raised by a bunch of bikers, but eventually Jackson and the rest of my Dads' won them round. I look round the room to see if I can spot them, but Chastity shakes her head, realizing what I'm seeking.

"Dad's not feeling so good, sorry. They sent you a gift though." Chastity drags me over to a table laden with gifts. It's overflowing with packages of all shapes and sizes. I shake my head. I don't need presents, this party is more than enough for me, being surrounded by family and friends.

"Later," I tell her and turn to gesture at the bar, "this girl needs a drink first." No sooner have I said the words than hands grab me from behind and I'm pulled back into a hard chest.

"Fear not fair maiden, your savior is here." A hand appears in front of me bearing a glass of Fireball.

"Why thank you kind sir," I turn quickly planting a kiss on

my cousin Ryan's face. Chastity stands awkwardly beside me, staring a little too hard. She's had a crush on Ryan for as long as I can remember.

"Happy birthday cuz, hope you're enjoying your party now you've finally arrived." I look at my watch, as I thought I was right on time. Typical that my family couldn't wait for me to arrive before they started partying, but it doesn't matter, I'm just happy to see so many of them here.

"Shh you drunkard, you remember my friend Chastity?" I turn to introduce her, grinning when I see the blush heating up her face. She's so transparent, but Ryan should be used to it. He's a womanizer through and through. He's just left the military after a pretty gruesome time in Afghanistan, and I'm hoping he'll come home to us and settle down, although I suspect his mother wants him to move back to her in Perth, the other side of the country from us. As a child I grew up with Ryan, his Mom is Jackson's sister, but she left to follow her husband when he joined the military and didn't come home when she was widowed.

"I remember her, how could I forget a beauty like her." Ryan's charm is seeping from his pores. He should bottle it, he'd make a fortune. Chastity is simpering beside me. Eugh. Grabbing my drink from Ryan I decide to leave them to their mutual appreciation. They're practically undressing each other with their eyes. It's no good my telling her he's bad for her, she's old enough to make her own mistakes.

I've barely made it across the room when everything goes

to shit. Bobby behind the bar has the gatehouse phone in his hand and is shouting for Jackson. Apparently, there's someone at the gate who isn't on the guest list. We've got nothing to hide here, but there's a hell of a lot of money and time invested in the bikes in the bike shed so no one gets in or out without going through the gate which is manned 24/7.

"Who is it?" Jackson shouts across the room, his voice booming over the loud music.

Everyone stops what they're doing when Bobby replies, his voice full of disbelief.

"She says she's Rebel's mother."

CHAPTER THREE

Rebel

The music stops as every head in the place turns to look at me, meanwhile Jackson is striding over to the door with a look of fury on his face.

"Let's get the party going," I shout, desperately trying to ignore what might be happening outside. My heart is thundering in my chest. I can't lie, a part of me has wanted this day to come, but it's such a tiny part of me that it's overwhelmed by the thought of what this could do to my dads'. They're the ones who raised me after all. If that woman outside is who she claims to be then she's nothing more than an egg donor she's certainly not worthy of calling herself a mother.

The music kicks back in but the atmosphere is lost. It's bad enough that she turned up at all, but to choose tonight when I'm supposed to be celebrating with my friends and family just rubs salt into the wound. Chastity and Ryan appear at my side, both wearing looks of concern that I don't want to see. A part of me wants to go outside and see this intruder, but I refuse to let her ruin my night. I grab hold of my friends and pull them towards the makeshift dance floor, not giving them a chance to say no. The tension in the room diffuses a little as we sway in time to the music and a few others reluctantly join me.

Jackson seems to take forever before he comes back into the clubhouse and when he does his face gives nothing away. Eyes follow him as he seeks me out, his hand on my arm encouraging me to move to a quieter corner of the room.

"What... who...?" I stutter the words out.

"Don't worry about it tonight darlin'," he reassures me. "I've sent her packing, but we need to have a chat tomorrow and see how you want to handle this."

I'm torn, I want to run after her and ask her for answers but I'm not sure if I can look her in the face; this is the woman who abandoned me. I nod my head in agreement and feel Jackson's strong arms pull me into his embrace.

"Now, let's get back to your party," he whispers in my ear. "Head up, paste a smile on, let's show these guys how it's done." Jackson has always been able to pull me out of a funk, and I take his advice. It's my party and I should be celebrating.

I look around the room and remind myself that this is what

matters to me, these people, this home. I return to the dance floor, rejoining Chastity and Ryan. Chastity seems oblivious to the cheesy dad dancing coming from Ryan, she's too besotted by him to notice. I grin to myself; the girl has it bad, and I need to warn her off for her own protection. Ryan will eat her up and spit her out, leaving her heartbroken in the process. It's who he is and what he does.

The music changes to a rock ballad and I see Jackson join the dancing throng, followed by a woman I don't recognize. That's interesting. I wonder who she could be, there's a familiarity between them that tells me she's not a stranger to him, although she is to me. He looks happy though, so I leave him be, I can interrogate him later.

It doesn't take long before I'm a hot and sweaty mess, I've danced so much my feet are throbbing and I know I'll feel it in my calves tomorrow. Drinks keep appearing in my hand but I'm merry rather than drunk. I need to keep it that way. I make my excuses and head over to the bar where I know I can get a bottle of water to rehydrate with.

With my back against the bar I look out over the main room of the clubhouse and smile. Everyone is here that should be and they're having a ball from the look of it. There's a lot of bad dancing out there, but every face is lit with joy and laughter. That's what it's all about. I can't help the nagging voice that wonders what tomorrow will bring and how it could change everything, and I'm annoyed that I'm feeling this way. She doesn't deserve a second thought, she never gave me one after all. Chastity spots me and gestures for me to return to join her, she's still dancing, and I have to admire her energy and her rhythm. She's a much better dancer than me. I finish my water and head back out there, it's time to party again.

Jackson

I cannot believe the nerve of that woman showing up tonight of all nights. I'm furious and struggling to hold it in. I can't let Rebel see how much it's affected me. As soon as I saw her, I recognized her, she's married to a local statesman and her face is always in the papers. She looked so out of place out there in her navy twinset and pearls I almost laughed. Then I saw her eyes and I swear Rebel was looking back at me. I don't scare easily but realizing that this probably was Rebel's mother freaked me out. I can't lose my daughter, I love her too much. She's such a huge a part of me now, like breathing. I know that we're all her dads' but there's always been a special bond between me and her ever since the day I first held her.

I agree she has a right to be heard and Rebel deserves that, she needs to know why her mother would be so callous as to abandon her, and why she's taken so long to come back and ask for a place in her daughter's life. That's what she's after. The nerve of the woman, expecting to just walk back in and become a mother again.

I need to hold this anger back, before Rebel notices. She keeps throwing glances my way, checking on me. She's got that inquisitive look on her face and I can see its aimed at my dancing partner. I haven't introduced them yet; the time hasn't been right. I'm not sure yet whether it ever will be, I've never brought a woman into Rebel's life as there hasn't been one I wanted to make a permanent fixture and I won't force Rebel to suffer my latest fling if it's not going to go anywhere.

The ballad ends, and I shake my head at Sue when it's replaced by a fast track, she understands and follows me to the bar where I grab us both a fresh drink.

"Was it Rebel's mother?" she questions, taking a sip of her gin and coke.

"I think it was." I reply slowly.

"What are you going to do?"

"It's not my call, its Rebel's," I respond, gripping onto my beer so tightly I'm at risk of breaking the bottle. "I'll talk to her tomorrow and see if she's ready to meet her."

Sue says nothing, just nods her agreement before dragging me back onto the dance floor when another ballad comes on. I'll worry about all this tomorrow, tonight is Rebel's night and I need to make sure my girl enjoys her party. And tomorrow... I'll deal with whatever it throws up.

CHAPTER FOUR

Rebel

I'm supposed to have been sharing my room with Chastity, but when I wake there's no sign of her. I reach for my watch and groan when I see how late it already is. I've slept away most of the morning, but in my defense, it was a late finish. Looking over at the other twin bed it looks like it hasn't been slept in. I hold back a groan, hoping like hell she wasn't stupid enough to fall for Ryan's charms. I can't help the chuckle when I realize I'm treating her more like I'm her mother than her best friend. She's a grown up and old enough to make her own mistakes.

Showering helps rid my head of that drowsy clouded feeling that tends to follow a good night of partying, and I dress quickly in jean shorts and a strappy vest along with my white Vans before heading off in search of coffee.

The main area is back to normal, you'd never guess we

were partying till the early hours from the look of the room although the table full of gifts is still sitting in one corner. Armed with a coffee I head over and start reading the gift cards. One present sits off to the side on its own, the hand-writing doesn't look familiar and I almost drop the small parcel when I read who it's from... my mother! What on earth is she doing sending me a gift. I'm tempted to toss it in the waste bin unopened, but I know Jackson would tell me off for being impolite. I've been brought up to send thank you notes for gifts and taught to include a reference to the gift, so I guess I'll have to open it. I put it at the back of the pile, I'm not in any rush to open this particular one right now.

"Hey, baby girl," Jackson's voice enters the room before the rest of him. I rush over to him and envelop him in a bear hug. Right here, in his arms, is home. He crushes me back, then lifts me so my feet leave the floor and swings me round. "Whoah, you weigh a bit more than you did the last time I did this," he grumbles, but I can still hear the affection in his voice.

When he puts me back down, I stand there, hands on my hips and face off at him. "Are you calling me fat?" I screech.

Jackson almost doubles over with laughter and can't get his words out for a moment or two. "I'm not that bloody brave!" I give him my best death stare as that answer didn't do anything towards denying my suspicions. "Baby girl, you look beautiful." His reassurance is paired with a kiss to my forehead. He's winding me up, and like always, I bloody fell for it. I shove his shoulder and growl at him which just makes him break out in full on laughter.

"Good job I bloody love you!" I huff at him. He pulls me back into our hug and I enjoy the feeling of being wrapped in his arms. I love my independence, but I also love my family. I'm lucky that I have the best of both worlds.

"We need to talk." His voice has turned serious and so has his face,

I grimace in response. "I know, but not yet, later," I offer. "After I've opened my presents."

Jackson eyes the pile of gifts behind me and whistles, "Someone's a lucky girl."

He's right, I've been spoiled rotten by my friends and family. I can't help the huge grin that lights up my face.

"What are you waiting for?"

I look around the room, still not seeing who I'm looking for. "Have you seen Chastity?"

Jackson shrugs his shoulders in response, "Not seen her since the party." He doesn't look concerned, and I suspect he would if he thought Ryan had been messing with her, so I feel a little better. Hopefully I have nothing to worry about, but I know how much of a charmer Ryan can be. I also know he has no plans for sticking around and Chastity is looking for permanent, not a quick fling.

It's quieter than I'd expected for a Saturday morning, but then I did stay in my bed a lot later than normal. I guess the old folk are better at recovering from partying than I am, let's face it they've had a lot more years of practice than I have.

James and Harry, the new recruits, walk through the main room carrying black plastic bags of rubbish. In a normal MC they'd probably be described as prospects, but that's not how Hellion works. They're both a lot younger than me, and neither have been in the military unlike the rest of the guys. I think they come from broken homes and ended up here as they had nowhere else to turn without ending up at risk of a criminal record.

"You guys seen Chastity?" Jackson calls after them. James blushes red as a beetroot at the mention of her name but both shake their heads in response. Poor James is so sweet, and so innocent, I think the poor boy is still a virgin. He's the epitome of a high school geek, all lanky and lean with some pretty bad acne. He has the most amazing eyelashes though, I wish mine were that long. They're so wasted on a guy.

"Someone looking for me?" Chastity strolls in looking a tad worse for wear, and worryingly she has Ryan in tow. I give him my best death glare, but he just shrugs his shoulders at me. Chastity is oblivious and the closer she gets the worse she looks.

"I need coffee," she groans as she falls onto the nearest sofa, patting the seat beside her to indicate she wants me to join her. Ryan offers to freshen mine up at the same time, it would be rude to refuse so I pass him my mug. I'm grateful he's going to be out of earshot, so I can give my friend hell for her bad decisions.

"Nothing happened," Ryan keeps hold of my hand and looks me in the eye, so I can see the honesty in his words. "She drank too much so I took care of her. I didn't want her to ruin your party." Bless him, he's not the dog I had him down for.

"Thank you," I whisper in response.

Sinking down on the sofa next to Chastity I nudge her shoulder and wink at her. "So, whose bed did you crawl out of this morning." I use my best stern voice on her, I'm going to have fun with this situation.

Chastity flushes like she's embarrassed and can't look me in the eye. Oh dear, I don't think Ryan's told her that he was a gentleman last night. This could be interesting. She tries to start a conversation several times but each time she falters. I have to put her out of her misery when I see her eyes well up.

I've never seen her look so relieved as when I tell her Ryan didn't sleep with her in that way. "Oh, thank god," she sighs.

Ryan chooses that moment to return and looks like someone stole his puppy as he hears Chastity's response. "What the hell?" He sounds really hurt.

The next few minutes are hilarious as Chastity tries to talk her way out of her gaffe. Instead of making it better she makes it worse when she tells him she'd never sleep with him as he's such a male tart. Ryan looks hurt and I'm crying with laughter watching the interaction between them. It's like watching a cheesy virtual reality show. He eventually relents and puts her out of her misery by agreeing with her.

"Don't worry, Chastity. You didn't offend me really, you're right, I'm a tart and you're far too good for a player like me. You deserve much better than me beautiful girl." He places a peck on her cheek before squishing in between us and pulling us into a hug. Chastity slaps him on the arm, relief written all over her face.

"Besides, "Ryan splutters his coffee as he spots Jackson stalking towards us, "my uncle Jackson would kill me if I did anything like that."

"Too bloody right I would, don't you forget that my boy, you're not too old for me to put you over my knee and teach you some manners." Jackson laughs.

Jackson looks at the table of gifts then back to me. "Open your presents, Rebel. We still need to have that talk."

CHAPTER FIVE

Rebel

I t took me over an hour to decimate the pile of gifts. I've been spoiled rotten, there was everything from jewelry to bottles of Fireball in there. My friends and family know me well, sadly my mother obviously has no clue whatsoever as she bought me a string of pearls. They're classy and obviously expensive, but so far removed from my taste and style. I'm not sure what to do with them.

I can't put off my conversation with Jackson about her anymore and head outside in search of him. As I suspected I find him in the rear garden area. It's so peaceful out here, it's one of the places I come when I want to think. I grit my teeth and head over to take a seat on the bench beside him.

For a moment neither of us speaks. It's not exactly an easy

conversation to have. After a few moments of us both just sitting there Jackson finally breaks the silence.

"She wants to meet you." There's no indication from his tone as to how he feels about the situation. I know how I feel, I'm angry, nervous, frustrated and scared all rolled up into one. I'm not sure whether the lack of inflection makes me feel better or worse. He's the one I'm closest to and I think deep down I wanted him to shout and tell me that he wouldn't allow it, saving me from having to make the decision.

"Why? Why now?" I truly can't understand why it's taken her thirty years to decide she finally wants to know me. She abandoned me for fucks sake, that hurt is so deeply ingrained it's an essential part of who I am.

"I don't know," Jackson sighs. "She's adamant that she regrets leaving you…"

Before he can continue, I've interrupted him. "Abandoned me!" I shout out. "She abandoned me like a worthless piece of junk, let's not dress it up into something nicer by saying she left me." Angry tears are threatening, and my eyes are stinging trying to keep them at bay.

Jackson puts his arm around me and draws me in close. "I know baby girl, I know. But at the end of the day she is your mother. I guess that means you should at least listen to her." I can hear the defeat in his voice now. That woman has caused this, she's made this man who has loved and nurtured me since the day he found me, feel bad. She deserves nothing from me. I know though, that cutting her dead will hurt Jackson more. He's always been such a gentle natured soul, preferring to believe in the best in everyone.

I sag my shoulders in defeat. I'll meet her, but it will be on my terms and in a place of my choosing. Jackson accepts this when I tell him.

"What does she look like?" I wonder out loud.

"Honestly?" He chuckles as he recalls the memory of her from last night. "She looks like a society princess, don't get me wrong she's beautiful still, and she has your eyes, but that's about all that's in her favor. She looked like she was chewing on a wasp when she had to talk to me. I'm well beneath her station."

"Bollocks! She's lucky that you deigned to talk to her, stroppy cow." Jackson doesn't have to say anything, he just gives me the look. You know that look, the one that speaks volumes and lets you know just how much you've disappointed a parent. I sigh loudly, it's exaggerated and over the top, but it's how I feel about the whole sorry situation right now.

"Rebel…" he says quietly, but there's unspoken communication running through that single word.

"We'll have nothing in common and I'm pretty sure she won't like me if she's that stuck up." I protest.

"Everyone loves you, and you're used to awkward clients, just treat her like you'd treat one of them." Jackson advises.

"So, what did she have to say for herself?"

"Not a lot, she was a little put out that you hadn't come out to see her yourself, but I explained that it was your birthday party and that the time wasn't right. She clearly didn't want to talk to me, so she gave me her number and asked that I get you to call her to arrange to meet up." He looks at me and before I can voice the question, he's already answered it. "No, she didn't give any explanation other than she'd made a terrible mistake all those years ago and now she wants to make it right."

I'm not sure that she can make this right. How can you justify abandoning a child at all, never mind just dumping it at the gates of an MC. What if no one had come along and found me? I could have died.

Growing up my heritage was never hidden from me; my Dads' were open and honest about it. I guess they had to be as I'd been a handful when I was young and constantly asked questions about why my family was so different to everyone else that I went to school with. Back then most families were the standard Mum, Dad and 2.4 children. It was only as I grew older that I understood that there is no such thing as a normal family. They come in all shapes and sizes. There are single moms, single dads, same sex parents and kids being raised by grandparents or the state. They'd explained that my Mum wasn't able to look after me, but that they would all be there for me. They never showed me the note until my eighteenth birthday, as mature as I was, I don't think they thought I'd understand it properly any earlier. Truth be told, even now I'm thirty

I'm still not sure I understand it. I don't get how a mother could abandon her own child. She obviously wasn't ill, or from the sound of things even facing hard times. I've always interpreted it that I was just in her way.

Having a mother who abandoned me shaped me into the person that I am now. As much as I put on a brave face for the rest of the world, there's a deep part of me that will never feel I'm good enough. Don't get me wrong, I've had so much love and affection from the family that have raised me, but that can't ever outmatch the knowledge that she chose to leave me. She made that choice, it wasn't forced on her.

Jackson is still holding the card out to me that I presume has her phone number on it. I'm surprised to see that it's a business card when he hands it over. Mrs. Deidre Donahue. No title, just a phone number. It's obviously expensive, thick cream card with simple black text. Very classy. Very impersonal. Deidre Donahue, I roll the name around my tongue trying to picture what she will look like. I see nothing. There's nothing here to identify her. I feel no disappointment, if anything its relief. She's still anonymous to me other than a name. Distant and anonymous, it's how I'd like to keep things, but I know that I can't. Pandora's box has been opened and it's time to face the beast within head on. I've been raised to be a tough cookie and never back down from a battle. I can do this. As I keep repeating that in my head, I wonder who I'm trying to convince. It's certainly not working on myself.

I flip the card in my fingers, trying to buy a little extra time but it's no good. I need to get this over with, so I can get on with the rest of my life. I've already decided there's nothing she can say to me that will excuse what she did all those years ago. Rising from the bench I stand with determination, holding my head high. Let's get this phone call over with.

CHAPTER SIX

Rebel

I stare at the business card in my hand, still unsure whether to ring the number or just tear the card into shreds. A huge part of me thinks that destroying the card is the best idea, but I know that Jackson would be disappointed in me. There's also a part of me that wants to see what she looks like and hear her pathetic excuse for why she abandoned me. In my mind I cannot think of anything that could justify what she did to me. I know however that I need to be the bigger person here. If I follow my gut instinct and ignore her then there will always be a part of me that will keep on wondering. She doesn't deserve one single thought from me but ignoring her is harder said than done now. I pick up my phone and dial the number from the card, my hand shaking the entire time. I'm still at the club as I couldn't face ringing her from my house, that's my sanctuary and I won't allow her to taint that safe space for me.

The phone rings several times and I half hope that there will be no answer. I'm disappointed when it's picked up at the other end.

"Deidre Donahue. How can I help you?" Her greeting is emotionless, her voice refined. I could be talking to a doctor's receptionist from the lack of warmth in her voice. My skin breaks out in goosebumps when I hear her voice.

"This is Rebel, Jackson said you wanted to talk to me." I don't say that I'm her daughter because she doesn't deserve the inference that she is my mother.

"Oh, I'm so glad you called. I was hoping you would. Can we meet for a drink? I've got a lot to tell you and I really don't think that the phone is the right place for this conversation." Her voice still betrays no emotion. I wonder if she always sounds like this?

"I can spare you an hour, but that's all I'm afraid. I've got a lot on." I offer. An hour is more than she deserves. The sooner I get it over with the better for me.

"Wonderful," she responds and gives me the address of her country club. Why we couldn't just meet in a coffee shop like normal people I don't know. We agree to meet in an hour. I suppose I should grab a shower and get dressed, although I don't think she'll appreciate the outfit I'm going to wear. She may be a country club devotee, and whilst I can hold my own in there thanks to my profession, she's going to get the real me, tattoos and all. I lay out a pair of skinny jeans that are fashionably ripped, a chain belt and black strappy vest that will show my chest piece off to its full advantage. I'm looking forward to seeing the expression on her twinset face when she sees that.

The shower eases a little of the tension in my neck, it wasn't there before my party and I dislike her a little bit more because she's the cause of it.

THE VALET at the country club raises his eyes when I step out of my Kia. I can see a hint of amusement in there. I've added my heels from last night and some heavy eye make-up to my look, in this outfit I feel ready for whatever lies ahead. Drawing back my shoulders I raise my head high and walk inside. As I pass through the country club, escorted by an equally amused concierge I can see looks of shock cross the faces of the rather staid clientele. That's right people take a good look, I don't plan on coming back here again.

The woman I'm introduced to doesn't look like me, she's ash blonde for a start. I know Jackson said he could see me in her face but there's nothing about her that reminds me of me. She reeks of money, although I'll hold back on whether she exudes class as it's too early to make a judgement yet. She's wearing a simple white linen shift dress, she has good legs for her age I'll give her that, and she's wearing nude pumps with a sensible heel. Her makeup looks flawless, but heavy with a bright red lipstick and dark smoky eyes. Her fingers end in the same color varnish as her lipstick. There's not a blemish in sight and I can't help closing my hands in on themselves to hide the slightly chipped ends of my own nails. She gives off an aura of chill, that's the best way I can describe it. It's not natural, and I feel uncomfortable in her presence already. If this was a prospective client, I'd have trusted my gut instinct and found a reason not to work with her.

I flinch as she moves towards me and I think she's going to draw me into a hug. I stand there stiff and awkward, it's almost a relief when she air kisses both cheeks instead. She gestures to the seat opposite hers and I sink into it, finding myself slouching. I can hear Jackson's voice in my head telling me to sit up straight, but the petulant child in me ignores him. There's just the slightest pursing of her lips when she notices my posture, but I take that as a small victory. I don't like this woman, I can't put my finger on it, and I know that it's more than just the fact she abandoned me.

"I'm so glad you could come, darling." She'd better not call me darling again or I'll leave. I shrug my shoulders at her. For god's sake, I feel like a rebellious teen sat here in front of her rather than the confident thirty-year-old that I am. I don't bother replying. "I guess I owe you an explanation...," she starts. No shit Sherlock! That's an understatement if I ever heard one. "I made some silly decisions in my youth and I let my parents dictate my life to me." She stops talking to take a sip of tea from the delicate bone china cup in front of her, looking at me for a response. She gets none. "I rebelled in my youth," she titters as she says this, and I think I want to throw up. There is no way this woman in front of me knows anything about rebellion. Look at her, she's so refined its painful to watch. "My parents were overseas, and I spent a lot of time drinking and partying, enjoying my freedom so to speak." So to speak, who the hell uses a phrase like that? I still sit there in silence. "By the time I realized I was pregnant it was too late, and I was scared. There was no one I could talk to, nor turn to. When you came, I was alone. I think I'd hoped that by denying to myself I was pregnant that it would all go away, but it didn't. My parents were due home and I panicked, there's no way they would have understood, they had a plan all laid out for me and a child wasn't part of it, so I did what I thought was best. I left you with the MC." The whole statement lacked emotion or warmth, she could just as easily have been giving the waiter her menu choice. Taking another sip of tea, she looks at me, awaiting a response.

"I'm not sure what you want me to say to that?" I whisper, scared to use my full voice in this tranquil setting for fear that I'd shout the place down. "You calmly sit there and tell me you abandoned me because you panicked. So, what made you change your mind after thirty years? You had all those years in between to reach out, why now?" This is what confuses me more than anything, she had so many opportunities yet failed me.

"Because my father passed away last month, whilst he was alive, I couldn't acknowledge you. He'd have been so disappointed in me. I'm sorry, he had very high expectations of me and I had to live up to them. It's what was expected of me."

"Did you love him?" She's still showing so little emotion I wonder if this woman understands love.

"I respected him, I believe I made him proud." Her response surprises me. She doesn't appear upset at his passing. I love and adore my dads' and can't imagine growing up without that. I don't believe I make them proud, I know I do because they constantly tell me. How sad that this woman obviously hasn't had that. That isn't enough to excuse what she did, the choices she made. It's not a good enough explanation, although I doubt that any explanation would satisfy me after so many years of feeling I wasn't good enough for her.

I promised her an hour, so I'll stay that long, but it drags. She tries to tell me about her husband, he's some kind of political wannabe, or that's how I interpret it. I have no brothers or sisters thankfully. That would have hurt more knowing she'd been a mother to them and not me. She seems to live her life seeking approval from society, she's definitely a lady that lunches. I doubt those neatly mani-cured hands of hers have ever done a day's work. Yes, she does charity work if you can call it that, organizing galas and receptions. Must be tough giving orders to the hired help then taking the credit for it all. Her life is so far apart from mine that I still feel like I'm sitting opposite a stranger when the hour is up.

"I'm afraid I need to go." I stand from the chair and nod at her, ready to take my leave.

"I'd like to see you again." She responds, holding her hand out to me. I take it and wish I hadn't. That's the fakest, limpest handshake I've ever encountered.

"I'll think about it." I offer, before turning my back on her and escaping this claustrophobic snobby environment as quickly as I can. I don't relax until I'm safely behind the wheel of my car. That was a truly horrible experience. As much as I don't want to repeat it, I can't disappoint Jackson. He'll expect me to be mature about this whole situation and polite. Letting out a scream of frustration I slam my hands on the steering wheel, catching the horn and startling the valet in the process. I shrug an apology at him as I drive off.

Why the hell did she have to come find me. I was fine exactly as I was. I didn't need a mother, and I sure as hell don't want the one that's found me. I decide to go home. I'll go back to the club later for my gifts and overnight bag. Right now, I just need the peace and serenity of my sanctuary.

CHAPTER SEVEN

Deidre

Closing the heavy front door and passing my handbag to the maid, I groan when I realize that Robert is home waiting for me. I can hear his voice coming from his study. I'd hoped to have a little longer to brace myself for the confrontation I'm sure is ahead of me.

Robert was my father's choice for me. The marriage that he expected me to make, so that through Robert I could fulfill my father's frustrated political aspirations. He'd never shied from telling me that he was disappointed that he ended up with a daughter rather than the son he'd always wanted. I was a poor consolation, a tool to be used to his advantage, and not deserving of his affection. My mother wasn't much better, I'd been raised by a succession of nannies and only wheeled out when society demanded it at a string of fancy dinners and charity lunches. I was as much a part of my mother's wardrobe as her pearls, although I suspect she held more affection for them than me. I guess it's no surprise I don't know what love is as I never had any growing up, and this has definitely been a loveless marriage of convenience.

I'd been happy to forget those few months of happiness and rebellion in my late teens when I'd been left home alone while my parents went on a grand tour of Europe. What good did remembering do, it was better left alone. Then my good for nothing husband made one too many mistakes and ended up owing the wrong people. Now I have to betray my own flesh and blood to save him. There's a bitter taste in my mouth at the thought of what lies ahead. I have no choice as he so bluntly reminded me. It's that or lose everything. Looking round the elaborately furnished home I share with him I realize that I have to comply. I cannot lose this, my place in society, my reputation and standing. They are all that I have, they are what identify me. Without them I am nothing, and worse, I'd be a nobody. I no longer have my father to support me, although I don't think in the last thirty years he ever once took my side against Robert. Instead he bailed Robert out of one mistake after another, reminding me that my place was beside my husband, regardless of the lies and cheating. Who was I to argue, Robert was made in my father's image as my mother constantly reminded me. It was my duty. My life was to be dedicated to Robert and the pursuance of his political career. My thoughts and feelings were unimportant.

There were days when I envied Rebel her freedom, the

obvious love bestowed on her by everyone at the MC. I'd checked in from a distance from time to time, just to make sure she was okay and being looked after. I wanted her to live life free of the chains and obligations I was enmeshed in. I'd naively thought my secret was safe, I was wrong. My father had his spies in the house the whole time he was away, he knew my dirty secret and he used it against me every time I tried to break free. He shared it with Robert, and over the years any spirit I had was broken down and destroyed in order to save the little girl I'd abandoned. I couldn't love her, it was too dangerous for her. Instead I had to pretend an apathy, to distance myself from any emotion in relation to her. My father and Robert wouldn't hesitate to destroy her, especially in the pursuance of their goals. I'd hoped that with my father's death I'd have been free, but no, Robert took over my father's mantle, there can be no escape for me. My mother will be no port of safe harbor, even now my father has gone she continues to take his side. It is so ingrained into her.

The study door opens before I can reach the grand staircase, the click of my heels obviously betraying me. "Get in here." Robert commands. He's long since given up the pretense of affection within our home. Only outside of these four walls will he play the loving husband.

"How did it go? Did she agree?" He's blunt and to the point. I bite back the angry retort, knowing that it will just lead to violence.

"I didn't get chance to ask her. I told you, this isn't going to be a quick fix. I need to earn her trust first."

Robert slams his fist on the heavy oak desk, scattering pens and papers to the floor. "You stupid bitch, we don't have time for your games. If we don't get her onside you realize we'll be ruined!"

"This isn't my mess, Robert. I'm trying my best to fix it." I reply quietly, knowing as soon as the words leave my mouth that it was a mistake. He rushes towards me gripping my wrist tightly, twisting the skin until it burns.

"You stupid idiot, what have you been told about answering back!" He slams his other fist into my stomach. Again, and again until I slump, unable to stand from the pain radiating through me. Robert is like any clever abuser, he never leaves obvious marks, instead choosing to hurt me where it cannot be seen. The scariest thing is that the longer we are together the more he seems to enjoy abusing me, debasing me. Outside our home he is the perfect gentleman, inside it he is an unspeakable monster.

I've been drawn into this plot against my will, knowing if I don't comply then my daughter will be sacrificed for his greed and amusement. My only chance of saving her is to befriend her, earn her trust and betray her. It isn't much of a choice, but it is the only one that I have. The price of not agreeing is too high. Even if I were to take the cowards way out and sacrifice my own life, she won't be safe. Robert has begun hinting that he'd like her in his bed, and there is no way I could subject her to that. He is sick and twisted. He destroys everything he touches. This ruse is the only way I have of keeping her safe, but I need more time than he is allowing me.

"I'm sorry," I sob out. I learned many years ago not to cry, it just makes him angrier. It's like my tears fuel his violence. "I'll try harder."

Robert looks at me, his face full of disgust, before releasing my trapped wrist and allowing me to drop to the floor in a heap. "Get out of my sight you worthless slut," he hisses at the same time he kicks me in the stomach for good measure. He turns his back on me, not caring if I crawl or walk away from him. He's made his point clear and I am no longer worthy of his attention.

Each step on the staircase hurts, all I can do is grit my teeth and pray to a god that has never listened to me before to save my daughter from this crazy man. Entering my room, the maid already in there gives me a look of sympathy, before helping me to step out of my dress. She's drawn a hot bath for me and I sink into it with relief. This is a ritual that has gone on for as long as I can remember. The staff witness the abuse, stay tight lipped and do what they can to make it easier for me to recover. They're paid well for their silence and acceptance. I'm under no illusion that they do any of this for me. It's all for him. It's the price we all have to pay.

CHAPTER EIGHT

Rebel

I'm torn and confused. I'm not sure how I should be feeling right now. I've spent the afternoon on my sofa trying to watch TV and it's not working. I can't concentrate. I know that Jackson is going to be waiting on my feedback from this morning. I owe him that, but I don't know how to begin to explain it to him. For god's sake, I can't even concentrate on an episode of Criminal Minds, a show I normally love. I've tried herbal tea, I've tried sitting in my garden and appreciating the tranquility, I've tried everything short of drinking and right now I know if I open that bottle I won't stop until I'm a mess.

Jumping up from the sofa I grab my bag and car keys. I'm going to head back to the clubhouse and talk it through with Jackson. Regardless of any dilemma I find myself in he always finds a way of counseling me by asking me the right questions until I understand what I need to do, how I should respond. I think this particular situation may be a little out of our comfort zone for both of us.

Pulling into the clubhouse I realize that I miss the old days. When I was a child this place was always full of energy and excitement. Now the guys are older it's a lot quieter and more laid back around here. Most of them are now old enough to retire and they desperately need some young blood to join them. There's a massive age gap between the two young apprentices and the original gang. James is only 18 bless him and Harry is 22. Aaron the VP is probably the youngest after that and he's 55. There's such a contrast between the MC's you see in the news and on TV and what Hellion MC is. The younger generation tend to look for adventure and excitement and they're not going to find it here. The thought that the MC may be dying out saddens me.

I'm so lost in my thoughts I've no idea how long I've been sitting in my car, reminiscing about the past and worrying about the future. Jackson startles me by tapping on the driver's window to get my attention. I roll it down and smile at him in greeting.

"You planning on coming in or just sitting here in your car all afternoon?" He greets me with a laugh. He offers me his hand as I step out of the vehicle and I take it, grateful for the familiar contact. He looks me over, concern on his face. "That tough?"

I'm not sure how to respond. "It wasn't tough as such, but it's left me so conflicted."

He nods his head in understanding, pulling me into a hug. "Want to talk it through?" he offers.

"Yeah, that would be good." We head inside and to his office. I love this room, I've spent so many hours in here with him, watching, learning, talking. It's a place that feels comfortable and safe.

We sit beside each other on the worn leather sofa, coffees on the table in front of us. Leaving mine untouched I try and describe my meeting with Deidre. I still can't bring myself to call her my mother, I'm not sure I ever will.

"We both knew it was going to be awkward," Jackson reminds me. "It's still early days and I think you need to take this slowly. Baby steps," he suggests.

"I guess." I brush my hair back from my eyes and look at him. "I'm so torn. All my life I wanted her to show up, and now she has, I'm not sure I want to know her." I confess. "There's something I can't put my finger on, something just a little off about the whole situation."

"Your intuition is normally pretty good, "Jackson agrees with me. "But this time you've got a lot of emotions that might be clouding it." He's making a lot of sense to me right now. Perhaps for once my gut is wrong about this woman. Maybe I should give her a chance and try to get to know her.

We spend a little longer chatting until I feel more relaxed, more my normal self. We've discussed my concerns, and Jackson has reassured me that his love for me won't lessen just because my mother has come back into my life. He just wants me to be happy, and if that means having her around then he's fine with it. He tells me that she used to be fun.

"You remember her?" I'm shocked as he's never told me that before.

"She's pretty hard to forget." He smiles as he remembers. "That summer we'd not long come back from serving and we maybe did party a little too hard," there's a glint in his eyes that lights up his whole face. They're obviously good memories. "She was around a lot that summer, it was obvious she was a good girl rebelling against her upbringing, I think she said her parents were away. Back then we all used to get high a lot so quite a few of my recollections are hazy, and I think that's why she ended up sleeping with a few of us. I remember a lot of laughter, and a shit load of drinking." Suddenly he looks sad. "Then suddenly everything changed. One minute she'd been this fun-loving party girl, the next she was a stuck-up bitch who was too good for us. Things were said that couldn't be forgiven and she stormed out. I never saw her again until last night."

I'm shocked, Jackson knew who she was all along. He remembered her. Why didn't I know this? Why did she change so quickly? The way he described her doesn't fit with the woman I met today at all. I'm more confused than ever.

"Why did you never contact her?" I blurt the question out.

"Because we only knew her as DeeDee, never knew her

full name or where she was from. As you can guess we didn't move in the same circles, so none of us bumped into her after she left. I wasn't even sure it was her when I read the letter. I'm ashamed to say there were a few girls hanging around that summer." Jackson looks slightly abashed.

"Come on, you were young, you'd just left the army and you were all part of an MC," I say with a laugh. "You guys have never struck me as the Sons of Anarchy type, but I think you may have a little more street cred after what you've just shared."

Jackson looks quite proud of himself and I burst out laughing, I can't help it.

"Yeah, I guess this old dog had a few tricks up his sleeve." He winks at me.

"Wow, this last twenty-four hours has really messed with my head. Who knew turning thirty would be such a revelation. I think I'd like to go back to being twenty-nine again if that's okay with you. This is all a bit much to handle." This has been a total mind fuck for me and I think I'm more confused after this chat with Jackson than I was before it!

"Sorry, darlin'." he smirks. "Afraid you've got to grow old like the rest of us."

"Pffft." I respond whilst punching him on the arm. Ouch! That was a mistake, I'd forgotten how much strength he has in his arms, they're solid. Jackson just laughs at me.

"Come on baby girl, I think your friend Chastity could do with saving from that rogue of a nephew of mine."

Shit, I'd forgotten all about Chastity. I just hope she didn't do anything silly in my absence. Who am I kidding, that girl doesn't know how to behave. I let Jackson offer me his arm to raise me from the sofa and head off to find my best friend.

CHAPTER NINE

Rebel

It doesn't take me long to find Chastity, she's sitting in the lounge with Ryan, Bandit and his old lady Smokey. There's a lot of laughter coming from the table which doesn't surprise me as Bandit is a real joker. He's one of the older members but doesn't really act his age, when his grandchildren are here, he's the first to get down on the floor and roll around in the dirt with them. Bandit and his wife are a lovely couple, they've been together for ever from what I've heard. They were sweethearts before he joined up, then when he returned less of a man than he used to be she still stood by him. From the stories they've told me he tried his best to push her away, but she refused to give up on him, and look where they are now. This year will be their fortieth anniversary. It's kind of weird to think that they've been a couple longer than I've been alive, although he's often been heard to jest that he'd have got a shorter sentence for murder. Despite his protestations they're totally devoted to each other.

His nickname Bandit came about when he lost his arm in an incident before he left the military, it's why he tried to break up with Smokey, but she wasn't having any of it. Smokey apparently looked like Sally Fields when she was younger and of course Bandit wanted to believe he looked like Burt Reynolds and that's how they ended up with their nicknames.

I walk over to join them, standing behind him I place a kiss on top of Bandit's bald head. What he lacks on the top of his head is more than made up for by the bushy mustache and beard he sports, although now its peppered with grey. Smokey sees me and smiles warmly at me, whilst Bandit starts muttering.

"For god's sake woman, I know I'm a sex god, but please, stop hassling me whilst I'm with my woman," he jokes. "Which one of my harem is it today?" He turns in his chair to get a better look at me and his face lights up when he sees me. "Rebel, darlin', come give your old man a hug." He drags me onto his lap and wraps me in a huge embrace. I love this man so much. I stay seated on his lap and look around the table.

"So, what were you guys talking about?" I ask, pinching a mouthful of coffee from Bandit's mug.

"The old days when I met Smokey," Bandit says, a dreamy look on his face.

"I was asking him about his accident." Ryan looks serious. I know it's not long since he left the military and that it had been pretty traumatic. The vehicle he and his team had been traveling in had been blown up by an incendiary device and they'd lost a friend as a result. I try to recall what happened and think I remember him telling me that his friend had lost a leg in the incident then committed suicide after they returned home. A shudder runs through me, that could so easily have happened to Bandit if he hadn't had Smokey fighting to keep him with her.

"No need to talk about that." Bandit cuts him off. He won't talk about the incident, but he doesn't mind talking about his recovery. Ryan is fascinated with how Bandit overcame his disability, not that we're allowed to call it that, he calls it his inconvenience. I guess that's how he manages to get through each day.

I tune out of the conversation, lost in thoughts of my meeting with my mother this morning but my attention is drawn back to them when they start talking about him having to learn to use his left arm.

"Yeah, I was right handed so it was quite a learning curve having to get used to only being able to use my left arm, course I have it down to an art after all these years." Bandit grins as a certain memory comes back to him. "The best thing about losing my arm was that for the first six months it felt like someone else was jerking me off." He guffaws with laughter at the same time that Smokey punches him in the arm.

"Bandit! How many times do I have to tell you not to share

that information!" She chastises, at the same time she's trying not to laugh. Ryan and Chastity are doubled up with laughter, that's probably the first time they've heard the story. I've heard it a lot, although it still makes me smile.

Bandit runs his hand through his full beard and looks to be deep in thought. "More times than I can recall, sweetheart, but you still love me." He flashes a cheeky grin at her and my heart melts at the look of adoration that passes between them. He reaches for her hand and places a kiss on it.

"Aww you guys are so sweet." Chastity gushes. I laugh at her, but she's right. They make a great couple and I'm a little sad that I don't have a guy like Bandit in my life. I just haven't met the right one yet. I guess part of my problem is growing up with some of the couples here at the MC, they are really tight, and I want that in my life. I've yet to find anyone who comes close to offering what I'm looking for.

Jackson is in no rush for me to settle down, he's often told me he doesn't want to have to share his baby girl with a guy that isn't good enough for her, and in Jackson's eyes I'm not sure any guy would meet his requirements. The men in this MC are a hard act to follow - good looking, caring, respectful and strong. The guys I've met never quite hit the mark. Still, who needs a man when I have Netflix and Ben and Jerry's to keep me company.

"Did you go meet her?" Smokey looks at me and asks the question the rest of them were too hesitant to voice.

"Yeah," I hesitate. "She's not what I expected." I confess.

"In what way?" Chastity asks.

"I guess in my head after all these years I've built her up into some kind of evil witch, whilst secretly hoping she'd be more like my fairy godmother. She's neither. I can't get a handle on how she makes me feel, but something's not right." I offer.

"It's early days darlin'." Bandit reminds me. "It's been a hell of a shock to us all, we're here for you." He rubs my arm to reassure me. Everyone around the table echoes his sentiment.

I'm so fortunate to be a part of this family who always have my back. I don't know what I'd do without them. They've allowed me the freedom to become the person I wanted to be, supporting me all the way, even when they didn't agree with some of the decisions I've made. They were really against me moving out and living on my own, but they've come to terms with it now. I guess in their eyes I'll always be that little girl that they cradled in their arms.

"That conversation got a bit deep," Chastity grins. "I say we go back to Bandit telling us more of his adventures!" Smokey groans at the prospect, but secretly I know she loves hearing his stories as much as I do.

We pass the rest of the afternoon in laughter. All days should be like this.

CHAPTER TEN

Deidre

R obert is furious with me. It's been a week since my meeting with Rebel and he's pushing for things to progress. He doesn't understand the subtleties, I can't just barge in there. It's obvious that she has no interest in building a relationship with me, and why should she. After all, in her eyes I'm the woman who callously abandoned her. She has no idea of the motives behind that, or of the nightmare that my life is. I can't lie, a huge part of me wants to play no part in this cruel deception. There can't be a good ending in this for Rebel, and there sure as hell won't be a happy ending for me.

I turn my attention back to the gala dinner plans that are in front of me and groan when I see the name of one of the attendees. My daughter has purchased a ticket for the charity event this weekend that I am organizing. In all the years I have been running these events she's never attended. Why does she have to suddenly start now? It's a fundraiser for a local children's home. I guess I should have known she'd have a soft spot for abandoned children, being one herself. I'm worried that I won't be able to keep her safe if Robert finds out. A thought runs through my mind, and I want to dismiss it out of hand. What if I were to tell Robert that she'll be there. It might give me a little breathing space, and if I'm really lucky, save me from another beating. They've become much more frequent since this whole mess started. It's getting harder to cover up, whilst the bruising isn't obvious I'm carrying myself much more stiffly these days in an attempt to reduce the constant pain, not to mention popping painkillers like sweets. I guess I don't really have a choice. If he sees her there and I haven't told him then I'll be in a bigger mess than if I tell him. I slam my pen down in frustration, wincing as it snaps jaggedly in half and cuts my finger. A drop of blood lands on the sheet of paper below. It's an omen, it has to be, and not a good one. The name it has landed on is Rebel's.

ROBERT SEEMS DELIGHTED at this turn of events, I can see the wheels turning behind his eyes and I know that whatever he has planned will not be good. He'll find some way to hurt or humiliate my girl. I wish I could warn her, save her from what is to come, but there's nothing I can do. I learned years ago about the high price of disobedience when it comes to Robert. I'd gladly sacrifice my life to save her, it's what a mother does, but even that wouldn't be enough. Robert is cold and callous and won't stop until he has what he wants. If anyone gets in his way he'll bury them, quite literally. I've heard and seen more than I care to recall over the years. The older he gets the darker his tastes and proclivities and the more ruthless he becomes.

He finally realizes I'm still in the room and looks up in annoyance. "What the fuck are you doing here? Get out, I can't stand the sight of you, you ugly bitch!" he hisses. I startle at the venom in his voice, but I should be used to hearing it now. I'd rather hear the venom than his quiet voice. That's the one he reserves for when he's really humiliating me and taking it out on me. Even the thought of how he can be when he is like that makes me shudder.

"Yes Robert, sorry Robert." I almost whisper as I back out of his study.

"Christopher!" he bellows as I retreat. "Get your ass in here, I've got a job for you."

Chris

Robert is shouting for me again. Am I not allowed any fucking peace in this house. I detest the man, but right now he's paying the bills for my mother's expensive care home so I don't have a lot of choice. Shrugging my jacket back on I head off to see what he needs this time.

"Sit down, sit down." He indicates the chair in front of his desk, he's bristling with some kind of energy which instantly gets my back up, it's not always easy to tell which way Robert's moods will swing. Luckily for me Deidre is the only one on the receiving end of his temper so far. I've seen the way he treats her and it's disgusting, you'd get locked up if you treated an animal the way he abuses her, but so far he seems to have got away with it. Robert doesn't normally get his own hands dirty, unless he's doling out some punishment to his unfortunate wife. The rest of the time he has a team of lackeys, including me, to do it for him. I wonder what poor innocent he has set his sights on this time?

"I have a job for you," he smirks as he pushes a photograph across the desk to me. I pick it up disinterestedly until I see the subject. She's stunning. I can't help wondering what she's done to annoy him. "She'll be at the gala dinner this weekend. I want you to seduce her. Fuck her. Here…" he passes a tiny vial of liquid over to me. "Put this in her drink, she'll let you do anything you want to her once that is in her system." Fuck. I don't like the way this conversation is going. "I need you to make her submissive to you, she has something I want and you're going to help me get it."

I look at him, shock flooding my system. "You can't be fucking serious!" I protest. "I'm not a fucking gigolo."

"You're whatever the fuck I tell you to be Christopher. If you want me to keep paying your mother's fees then you'll do whatever I tell you to do without question." He slams his fist on the desk, anger making the veins on his forehead pulse. When he's like this you can see the monster within. You'd never guess he's the same politician the rest of the world sees, the baby kissing, hand shaking best friend of the community. What a two faced prick, but that's my father all over.

That's right, this dick is my father, although he's never acknowledged me. He raped my mother back when she worked for his father and as soon as he realized she was pregnant and planning an abortion he kidnapped her and imprisoned her until she gave birth to me. He kept us as his dirty little secret for years, allowing us to live on the bread line whilst he flaunted his wealth to the press every opportunity he could. The magnanimous benefactor of so many charitable causes whilst his own son went without food and clothes. Pompous prick. I was eighteen before I learned the truth, my mother's health was deteriorating and she decided to come clean in case she didn't make it through the treatment. The poor woman thought he'd acknowledge me and welcome me into his family. She couldn't have been more wrong, instead she sentenced me to a lifetime of servitude to the prick. Thankfully I don't think she'll be around for much longer, she'll finally be at peace and I can escape this shitty life and finally be myself.

CHAPTER ELEVEN

Rebel

My new dress is hanging on the wardrobe door and I keep admiring it. I've never been to a charity gala before but when this one was advertised as being in aid of the local children's home I knew I had to go. I wanted to give back, I know how those children feel. They've been abandoned by the people who should love and care for them, I was lucky that I had my dads' to raise me but these kids don't even have that. The theme of the evening is black and white and my floor length dress is all black, off the shoulder with a thin gauzy train at the back. Pinched in at the center it accentuates my bust and shows off my narrow waist to perfection. It's a sheath dress with a split up one thigh. I love it on the hanger, but it's one of those dresses that looks simply stunning when it's on. I feel a million dollars in it. Chastity is my plus one and has decided to contrast with me and wear white. Her dress clings to her like a second skin, a silvery sheen to the satiny fabric that really makes her eyes pop. I'm excited about attending, although I hope we don't end up with company that's too pompous. This is the kind of event my mother organizes after all. I'm pretty sure she'll be there. We still haven't spoken since our meeting, and I'm not sure what to say to her if I bump into her. There's just too much to think about, it's not going to be an easy decision to let her into my life. I push thoughts of her aside and head to the shower, I have a ball to prepare for.

I hand my car keys over to the valet and take a moment to admire the property in front of me. It's an old colonial house that has been converted into an event and conference center with accommodation. The subtle ground lights reflect back up on the property facade and give it a warm and welcoming feel. Chastity totters around the car towards me, squealing with excitement as she looks at the building.

"I'm so excited!" She grabs hold of my arm, linking it with hers. I'm a little concerned that she's wearing heels she can't handle this evening as she's teetering along like a baby deer taking its first steps. She was adamant that as she was my plus one she had to have the highest heels she could find. It was the only way she could compete with me as she knew I'd wear my favorite 5" heels. We head to the entrance that is warmly lit and welcoming and we admire some of the fashion choices entering before us. All the guys have gone for simple black dinner suits, apart from one. He's wearing black trousers and a white blazer. I think he's trying to look like a crooner from the Sinatra era, but to me he just appears creepy. He's on the receiving line and I gasp when I spot the woman standing beside him. It's Deidre. Despite her age she looks stunning. I can't fault the class that rolls off her and she's wearing a simple black sheath as well, although hers has thin straps. I guess the guy she's with must be her husband, although the way he's talking to her doesn't look very affectionate. If I didn't know better I'd swear he'd been snarling at her, although when he moves his lips away from her ear he pastes a huge grin on his face just as I step in front of him.

He reaches for my hand and draws it to his lips where he places a kiss on my fingers. I want to pull my hand back but that would be rude. A shiver runs through me, it feels like someone just walked over my grave. Instinctively I decide that I don't like this man who's grinning at me with an obviously fake smile as it doesn't reach his eyes.

"You must be Rebel," he gushes. "Your mother has told me so much about you." I look at Deidre in surprise, wondering what she could know about me to share with him. I'm a stranger to her after all. I could have sworn I saw her flinch when he said my name, but it must be my imagination. "I'm delighted to meet you."

The line in front of us is moving quickly thankfully and I move on to my mother who greets me with a genuine smile. "I'm so glad you could attend, thank you for supporting us." She beams back at me. I mutter a polite response and move onto the next person in the line.

"That was intense." Chastity laughs as we gratefully reach the bar. "I'm not sure I rate your stepdad." She grimaces.

"Don't call him that!" I raise my voice a little too loudly for the company we're in and look around to make sure no one overheard me. "He creeped me out, he's no relative of mine." I assert much more quietly.

The bar tender approaches us as its now our turn. Chastity asks for a champagne cocktail whilst I opt for a diet soda. I'm driving this evening and I never mix drinking and driving.

She raises her eyebrows at me in surprise. "Aren't you drinking tonight?"

"Nope, decided I needed to keep a clear head, I can't afford to get drunk and bid in the auction, besides the tickets and the dress cleaned me out. "I chuckle.

"Party pooper," she laughs at me. "Let's go see who we're sitting with." As we turn to face the room Chastity lets out a gasp. I follow her line of sight and understand. The guy in our line of sight is hot, panty dropping, knicker wetting hot. He looks just a little older than us and his dark blonde hair is tousled, sitting just short of his shoulders. He's wearing a black suit with a narrow straight black tie and the clothing emphasizes his strong arms and legs. He turns to acknowledge a greeting and I suck in a breath, he looks just as hot from the rear as he does from the front.

I tap Chastity on the arm to get her attention, she's practically drooling at him and a little obvious. "Put your tongue away girl," I grin at her.

"I call dibs!" She exclaims. Damn, I quite fancied him

myself, but our girl code means he's now off limits to me. That's a shame.

We find our table and sit down, greeting the other guests who are already seated. I don't know any of them and after polite introductions they return to their own conversations. The seat at the side of me remains empty, and Chastity is happily chatting to the man at the side of her. I'm only half paying attention to their conversation, he's some kind of photographer, when I feel movement on my other side. Turning to greet the latecomer I'm startled to see it's the blond god from earlier. Up close he's even more attractive and I think my ovaries may just explode. With his dark eyes and neat beard I instantly think of Thor from the Avenger's movies. He's got a similar look, did I mention I have a huge crush on Chris Hemsworth?

It's Chastity's turn to be introduced and she's almost lost for words, stuttering out her name. I can't help the grin that lights up my face, the poor girl is smitten and who can blame her.

"Hi, I'm Chris" he introduces himself to me. His voice… I'm screwed. I'll definitely be having inappropriate dreams featuring him tonight.

"Hi Thor, I'm Rebel." It's only when I hear Chastity and the rest of the table laughing loudly that I realize my mistake. Oh. My. God. I just called him Thor out loud! I silently wish that the floor would open up and swallow me, before wondering how early I can escape without being rude.

CHAPTER TWELVE

Chris

I hadn't expected her to be this beautiful. She's funny as well. I like her. That just makes my job that much tougher, although sleeping with her won't be a hardship. If I'd met her tonight and not known who she was I'd have wanted her in my bed. The fact that Robert has ordered it though, that leaves a nasty taste in my mouth as I finger the vial in the pocket of my dinner jacket.

I saw the look that passed between Rebel and her friend earlier at the bar. I've a feeling they decided between them that the friend was going to get me. I can't let that happen. I wonder how strong the girl code is between them, and how to overcome their ploy. It helps that the friend is sat next to another guy, I may have managed to get to the table before them and orchestrate that. That other guy is my colleague and I've asked him to distract the friend and keep her out of the way this evening. I can't afford to let anything deter my plan.

As I'd expect from events like this the majority of attendees are trying to play the one-upmanship game. Bragging about the size of donations, cost of jewelry or the designer label on the extortionately priced gowns they'll never wear again. Rebel and her friend Chastity are a refreshing change and our table frequently rings out with their laughter. She's earned a few disapproving glances at her chest piece, but personally I love her ink. It's obvious that she's comfortable in her own skin and she's holding her own against an extremely catty woman sat opposite her. The old dear on my left has a fantastically dry sense of humor and keeps cutting the bitch down, she's obviously been won over by Rebel as have the rest of the table.

Rebel's conversation is witty, intuitive and sharp when needed. She refuses to be drawn when the conversation turns to politics, instead responding that she thinks such personal opinions are best kept to oneself. Clever girl. Despite the amount of ink adorning her skin she exudes an aura of sophistication and class that I hadn't expected. Chastity meanwhile is starting to get a little loud, my colleague has been plying her with alcohol. Despite what feels like a gazillion courses the meal seems to have done little to counteract the booze. Rebel meanwhile has insisted on drinking soft drinks so she can drive home. I need to do something to ensure she spends the night in my bed, and reluctantly finger the vial again, waiting for my opportunity.

The serving staff have cleared the dessert dishes away and all eyes turn to the stage as the auction begins. Stupidly high amounts are paid for theatre tickets, spa days and vacations. Looking at the programme open in front of Rebel I see that there's only one item she has circled, a pair of petite diamond earrings. The bidding climbs quickly and she soon drops out, a sigh of disappointment leaving her very kissable lips as the cost exceeds her limit. Her mother may move in wealthy circles but I can tell this girl doesn't and I find that refreshing. Just as the gavel is about to go down I call out a high enough bid that the item is mine. I chuckle inwardly, Robert will be pissed as it's his money I'm bidding with, but he can afford it. I excuse myself to go and settle the bid and return to the table with the expensive jewelers gift bag in my hand, placing it in front of Rebel.

"But, I can't accept those!" She protests. "I don't even know you." She pushes the gift back towards me.

"I insist," I smile at her. "You've made what I thought would be an incredibly stuffy evening much more bearable." I push them back.

Manners override her reluctance and she politely accepts the gift from me. Her friend Chastity is now very much the worse for drink and swears loudly as she watches our interaction. "Holy Fuck! No one ever bought me a gift like that." The whole table turns and observes her now very drunken state, including Rebel.

"I think it's time I took you home," she quietly advises Chastity who protests rather loudly. Rebel offers me a look of apology. I shoot a sideways glance at my colleague who senses my anger straight away and offers to escort her home himself. There's a bit of to and fro between him and Rebel but she eventually capitulates. Thank fuck! My plan had almost been derailed there. We escort Chastity to the waiting car then I persuade Rebel to return to the gala and encourage her on to the dance floor.

She fits me perfectly, she's starting to tire and after a few dances her head drops to my shoulder as we move around the dance floor to Aerosmith's "I Don't Want To Miss A Thing". She knows the song word for word and quietly hums them to herself as I guide her around the floor. When the song finishes she looks up at me, a blush of embarrassment on her cheeks.

"I'm so sorry, I kind of lost myself there, I love that song." She apologizes.

"That's okay, I loved hearing you sing it. Shall we go get a drink?" I gesture to the bar. When she agrees I take her arm to escort her around the crowded dance floor, all the way fingering the vial in my pocket. It's time I made a move.

Rebel

I wake up with a bitter taste in my mouth and no idea of where I am. I know I'm not at home and this isn't the clubhouse. I'm alone in a huge bed with very rumpled sheets, in what looks to be an expensive hotel suite. I stretch out and realize I ache everywhere. What the hell did I do last night and why can't I remember? The thick curtains prevent light from entering the room and I can only see the shadows of furniture. What I really need is a bathroom, I've obviously been woken by the need to pee. Spying a door across from the bed I stand on shaky legs and make my way over to it. Where the hell are my clothes? Come to think of it, where the hell am I? The last thing I remember is dancing with Chris at the gala. I decide to answer nature's call which suddenly seems rather urgent, then I'll find a bloody light switch so I can locate my clothes and phone. I'm not even sure what time it is thanks to the dimness in here, and my watch isn't on my wrist.

I'm startled when I open the bathroom door to hear the shower running, the room full of steam. There's an outline of someone in the shower and I suddenly feel vulnerable and uncomfortable. They haven't noticed me entering and I can't wait, the need to pee overtaking everything including any sense of decency. What on earth? Why does that hurt so much? Anyone would think I'd had a night of hot sex. Wait… is that what happened? I try and piece together the evidence before me, I'm in a strange hotel room, there's someone in the shower and my body feels like I've enjoyed a hell of a sexscapade, yet I have no memory of any of it. Without thinking, so distracted by my lack of memory, I flush the toilet only to hear a screech from the shower.

"What the fuck!" Shit, I've just subjected whoever is in

there to a jet of cold water. It's a male voice, but I'm still none the wiser.

The glass door of the shower opens towards me and I freeze. Holy fuck! That is the hottest man I've ever seen. I scan down his body, past his well-defined abs and my eyes almost pop out of my head as I get lower. No wonder I'm sore, he's huge! I hear a tut and look up to see him watching me.

"Didn't you know it's rude to stare." He chuckles. "Morning darlin,'" he proceeds to greet me. I suddenly remember that I'm naked and try unsuccessfully to cover myself with my hands which makes him laugh out loud. He moves closer to me and just as I think he's about to kiss me he reaches around me for a towel, wrapping it around himself as he leaves the room. What the fuck? I spy a robe on the back of the door and quickly cover myself with it before heading back out into the bedroom.

"Who...what...?" I splutter out.

He looks at me, shock written all over his face. "Why the hell are you looking at me like you don't know who I am?"

"Because I don't." The realization has me sobbing and I sink to the floor, my legs no longer able to support me. What the hell happened to me last night?

CHAPTER THIRTEEN

Chris

Fucking hell, I didn't expect that. She genuinely has no memory of last night. I'm kind of offended as I know that was the best sex I've ever had, and I was pretty sure she was enjoying it too judging by the multiple orgasms she experienced. She's on her knees on the floor and crying. I've no idea how to reassure her, but head over and kneel down in front of her, careful not to scare her any more than she already is. I gently reach over and put an arm on her shoulder. She looks up at me, eyes full of fear and I feel sick. I did that. I put that expression there.

"Let's get you up, get some food into you and I think we need to talk about what happened last night." She says nothing, but lets me lead her over to the small dining table in front of the window. As she sits she pulls the robe tighter around her. Guilt hits me. I open the heavy drapes and sunlight floods into the room, she turns her eyes away, startled by the sudden intrusion of light. She holds a hand to her head and winces. I'm guessing she has a hangover as she did knock back a few shots last night before we came up to the room, but I wouldn't have said it was enough to have affected her this badly.

Whilst she's perusing the room service menu I quickly check my jacket pocket, sighing in relief when I find the vial still in the pocket, unused. I couldn't go through with Robert's plan last night, I desperately wanted to sleep with her, but only if that was what she wanted as well. She'd seemed merry, but definitely not drunk when we came upstairs and I'm confused as to how she has no memory of our night together.

"I'll have some toast and black coffee please," she requests quietly, "and some painkillers if you have any?"

"Not on me. I'll see what room service can come up with." I offer. Having placed our order I sit down next to her at the table and take hold of her hand, causing her to finally look me in the eye. "What's the last thing you remember?"

"I'm not sure…" she pauses, obviously trying to recall anything. "Dancing?" She asks it as a question.

"Yep, we were dancing, can you remember the song?"

She shakes her head, concern written across her face.

"Aerosmith ring any bells?" She's about to shake her head when something flits across her face.

"Possibly...I'm not sure."

"I've never seen this before, but I have heard about it." I have an idea. "You ever heard of alcohol blackouts?" She shakes her head. "You were on soft drinks most of the night, but once we left the dance floor you switched to shots. You did have quite a few." I offer.

She looks up at me in confusion? "Shots? What the hell was I drinking?"

"Black sambucca."

"Oh fuck!" She looks horrified. "Why the hell did you let me drink that?"

"Because that's what you asked for."

"I've never been able to drink that stuff," she sighs. "It always makes me ill."

"I didn't know," I apologize. "Look, there's a good chance that your memories of last night will come back to you. I hope they do," I chuckle, "personally I think they were bloody good memories, definitely worth remembering."

"What did we do?" She looks horrified.

"We had the best sex I've ever had," I tell her. " I have to say your blow job skills are legendary." I grin at the memory. Rebel however looks ill. She throws a hand over her mouth and rushes for the bathroom where I can hear her throwing up. I can't say it does my ego any good that she's throwing up as soon as I tell her she gave me a blow job. Deciding my ego needs to stay in check here I follow her to the bathroom and hold her hair back for her as she vomits. When she's finished she's so drained she just stays collapsed over the toilet. I dampen a washcloth and clean her face for her, then despite her protests lift her into my arms and carry her back to the bed where I lay her down gently. I've heard of alcohol blackouts but I've never seen one before. I've no idea what to do for her. Before I can grab my phone and see what Google recommends there's a knock at the door, it's room service. I tip the waiter and once he's left I return to the bed, a slice of toast in hand to try and tempt her to eat. I also bring a bottle of chilled water as I'm sure she'll be dehydrated. She declines the toast but allows me to assist her to take small sips from the water. She soon lays back against the pillow, exhausted. Her heavy eyes slowly drift closed and I allow her to doze. I'm sure sleep will be good for her right now. I grab my phone and google alcohol blackouts while she sleeps, not leaving her side of the bed. I'm not sure why but I feel a connection to this woman. I want to keep her safe. Somehow I think that isn't what Robert had planned for me.

Rebel

I have a feeling of deja vu as my eyes open and I'm back in the bed I woke up in earlier. I still have no memory of last night, however I do have a very vivid memory of throwing up and Chris carrying me back to the bed. Wait... that's new. I remember his name now. If I know his name, then surely that means that I know him? Looking to my side I see I'm not alone this time. Chris is laid on the bed beside me, he's asleep and I take a moment to appreciate the view. He looks so peaceful, his long blonde hair spreading out on the pillow around his head. I feel an urge to trace my finger down his chest and abs and for some reason that's familiar, like something I've done before. I resist. I don't want to disturb him. I'm grateful that his bottom half is still encased in a towel. I'm still wearing the robe from earlier. My head doesn't ache quite as much as it did, but I do feel grubby. Gingerly I place my feet on the floor, grateful when I can stand without feeling nauseous. I wonder if I can manage a shower, I know I'll feel better for it, as long as I don't pass out. Silently I make my way across the bedroom.

The shower wakes me up a little, I'm still slightly unsteady on my feet, but that could be the nausea. I use the hotel supplied shampoo and conditioner and give my hair a thorough wash. That makes me feel better, as does brushing my teeth. Drying my hair and body with huge fluffy towels I put my robe back on then head back into the bedroom where I collapse back onto the bed, exhausted. Chris is still asleep and as loathe as I am to wake him, I need answers. Answers that only he can provide.

Chris has rolled onto his front, his towel must have been loose as I am faced with the most kissable behind I have ever seen. This time I can't help myself and reach my hand out, gently caressing his fine ass. It's enough to wake him, he rolls over onto his back and gives me a huge smile.

"Well, hello." He sits up to face me. "I see you're looking much better." He leans in and kisses me. As his lips touch mine an explosion of memories hits me, and I kiss him back.

CHAPTER FOURTEEN

Chris

She kisses me back. Our tongues do battle, greedy and not able to get enough of each other, and then we break apart, breathing heavily, our chests heaving.

"I remember," she smiles coyly at me. Thank fuck!

"Are you sure?" I slowly pull her robe apart, letting it fall from her shoulders and giving me a view of her heavy breasts. "I think I may need to remind you a little more," I suggest as I finger her taut nipple, causing her to arch her head back and groan with pleasure.

"I think, I think that would be a good idea," she pants as I draw her breast into my mouth, teasing her nipple with my teeth.

I roll her onto her back, and straddle her legs, pinning her in place. Holding her hands above her head I nip and kiss her neck, teasing my way down her body. She tries to lift herself from the bed, pushing up into me, the tension in her body obvious. She can't move, and she curses me for restraining her. I love her foul mouth.

"I want to feel you," she complains. I release her hands and she exhales in relief, it's short lived though as I move my head down her body out of her reach. My hot breath heats her skin as I tease her with my tongue, never quite hitting her sweet spot. I lift her legs over my shoulders and lap at her opening, tightening my grip on her thighs. She tries to pull back right before the first orgasm hits as I nip her clit with my teeth. "Wow," she exhales. "I'm not sure I remember everything though, I think you'd better keep going." She grins up at me.

"Happy to oblige." I turn her over so she's laid on her front, trapping her legs between mine. I grab a condom and quickly sheath my cock with it, I'm so hard for her right now I just want to be inside her. I know she's wet and ready for me. I push in quickly, balls deep and am rewarded with a scream of pleasure. I wanted to take this slowly, conscious that she might still be sore from last night, but can't help myself, especially in this position. Keeping her legs trapped between mine I thrust as hard as I can, my balls slapping against her body each time. She feels so tight, and I know I won't last long in this position. That's okay. I plan on spending the whole day in bed with her, worshipping her body with mine until we're both too exhausted to move. She screams out her release and I follow. Fucking hell, sex has never been like this for me.

She fits me so well, it's as though she was made for me. There's no way I can let her go.

"Wow, that was, that was fucking amazing," she sighs, her voice full of exhaustion. She rolls onto her side and I spoon in behind her, holding her close.

"That was just the beginning, darlin'" I assure her.

"Beginning?" She laughs. "I think you broke my vagina!"

I chuckle, pulling her closer. I don't know what Robert has planned for her, but I do know that I'll do everything in my power to protect her from him. Her breathing has slowed down and evened out, knowing she's asleep I close my own eyes. I don't know about breaking her vagina, I think her vagina has broken my cock!

THERE'S excited chatter in the room, and it pulls me from the dream I was enjoying. Cracking one eye open I see Rebel sitting at the dining table. She's wrapped in the hotel robe again, her mobile against her ear whilst her other hand holds a forkful of melon that's in danger of flying as she gesticulates wildly with that hand.

"I'm fine, honest. I just decided to stay over last night, I had a few too many shots." I can't hear the question on the other end of the phone but I do hear the screech of horror when she answers "Black Sambucca"

"Never mind me, what happened to you last night?" She

questions. "Who did you go home with?" I'm guessing from the lighthearted conversation on this end of the phone that she's talking to Chastity. I sit up, suddenly alert, needing to hear this next part. Rebel looks confused, and I wish I could hear both sides of the conversation. "Who?" she repeats. "You sure he was a gentleman?"

I let out the breath I didn't know I was holding when it becomes obvious from the conversation that my colleague did nothing more than make sure Chastity got home safely. I'm relieved. I don't know the girl but she's important to Rebel, and that means that she's now important to me.

They chatter on about girly shit and I tune out, helping myself to some fruit from the breakfast trolley that we had ignored earlier. I'm starving. We've spent the whole afternoon exploring each other's bodies and I'm amazed my cock hasn't fallen off. It's never had so much use. I decide to leave them to their chatter and grab a shower. I don't know about Rebel but I desperately need some food. I need to restore my energy.

Rebel

I'm relieved that Chastity got home safely, albeit a tad guilty that I ended up sleeping with the guy she'd called dibs on. Apparently she'd hit it off with George last night, the guy that had been sitting next to her and decided she'd try her luck with him as Chris was so obviously smitten with me. I'd have laughed at her if my body wasn't currently reminding me just how attentive he'd been. George had been too much of a gentleman to take advantage of Chastity in her drunken state, much to her disgust, and he'd also failed to leave her with his phone number. "Story of my life," she muttered at me.

"There's someone out there for you, I'm sure," I reassured her.

"Yeah right, remind me again why I have to wait for Mr. Right instead of enjoying the carnal pleasures of Mr. Wrong," she laughed.

"Because you're a good girl like me," I responded.

"Yeah right, some good girl you are. Tell me, are you home yet?" Sometimes the bond Chastity and I have is a little too intuitive, like now.

"Well, ermm, no." I confessed.

"You do know what time it is? And I don't recall you taking a change of clothes." I realize I have no idea of the time and pull the phone away from my ear to see. Oh hell, it's almost five! She's right, the only clothes I have are the ones I wore to the gala last night. "Want me to drop you off something suitable?" Chastity is the kind of friend everyone should have.

"I'm not sure what the plan is yet, can I get back to you?" I don't want to be too presumptuous. This thing with Chris is very new, and if I'm honest, he's not given me any indication that he wants it to continue after today.

"Yes, and I expect all the details, so be prepared to spill." Whilst Chastity has always been happy to give me blow by blow details of her sex life, I prefer to keep mine under wraps. She knows me better than that, but she will expect something from me.

"You know me better than that," I respond. "Anyway, I have to go, I can hear him coming out of the shower." We exchange goodbyes with a promise for me to let her know when I get home.

The bathroom door opens and I lick my lips at the sight of Chris, fresh from the shower. I don't think I'm going to be heading home any time soon.

CHAPTER FIFTEEN

Deidre

I think Robert is losing it. He seriously believed that getting Chris to spend one night with Rebel would accomplish his goal. The man has no concept of how relationships work. He's worse than a toddler. He really thinks he can snap his fingers and everything he wants will come to him. He's in for a rude awakening. Not that I'm going to be the one to tell him that. My ribs are still sore from the last beating.

I understand that he's under massive pressure to pull this deal off, but negotiation is a fine art. Perhaps he should have thought of that before he got so heavily into gambling. He's as bad at gambling as he is at being a husband. This time he lost money to the wrong people. They're not the sort to go quietly if the debt isn't paid. It would be easier to find the money he owes, even though I know he has none, than to accomplish what they are asking.

Chris just had his head bitten off, I could hear Robert's displeasure from out here. I cringe when I hear the turn of conversation. This is my daughter they're so casually discussing, and there's nothing I can do to help her.

"You'd better have fucked her, you lazy piece of shit!" Robert bellows. I can't hear Chris's response, it's too low to make out the words although it sounds like a conciliatory tone.

"I don't give a shit about her feelings, you have a job to do and I want it done." There's a crashing sound from the study and I suspect it's the contents of Robert's desk. The man has a violent and short temper. Again I strain to hear Chris's response, although when Robert once again threatens to stop paying the medical fees I can't fail to hear the slam of the door as Chris leaves the room. He sees me standing in the hallway and gives me a look of sympathy. He knows. He's seen the way Robert treats me behind closed doors. I can't stand his pity, we're both Robert's victims, just in different ways. I can only stay strong if no one cares. It's how I'm used to living.

"He's losing it, Deidre. I'm worried about what he'll do to Rebel." Chris confesses. I can see in his eyes that he's fallen for her.

"He won't hurt her, he needs her to sign." I reassure him, although what he'll do to her once she's signed is up for debate. He has an evil streak, and there's a good chance he'll do something to her for making him wait. I don't know what I can do to protect her from him when he's like this. These past few months he's unraveled so much, he's worse than he ever was. My body is proof of that. I don't think I've not been covered in bruises for at least three months. It used to be just a few times a year he took his rage out on me, now it's almost a daily occurrence. I'm not sure how much longer I'll survive the beatings or his rage.

Chris shakes his head, looking crestfallen as he leaves the house. I feel so powerless, there's no one I can turn to for help, no one who would have my back. Robert's made sure of that, isolating me from anyone I might forge a relationship with from day one, ably assisted by my father. I hope dear daddy rots in hell. I just wish Robert would join him there.

I think I've escaped Robert's attention and am quietly heading for the sanctuary of my room when his voice fills the hall, demanding my attendance. I shudder, knowing that another beating lies ahead. I open the study door, and brace myself before entering. This is my life, there is no escape.

Rebel

Chastity sits on my sofa, spitting out popcorn and giggling as I tell her about my night with Chris. We're supposed to be watching a movie, but she's not stopped grilling me since she arrived. Her excuse is that she's got to go home tomorrow so needs all the gossip now before she goes back to her dreary real life, especially as her evening ended on a low.

She knows that I'm not the kind of girl to kiss and tell so is trying to trick information out of me by asking ridiculous questions to see if I'll bite. It doesn't work. I've got my professional face on, one I've worked hard to perfect. I can think my client is the greatest idiot in the world, but I'll never betray that with my expression or emotions. The girl can't win. It helps that I spent a lot of time playing poker with my dads', any sign of weakness meant I lost, and I'm not a good loser.

"I don't want to go back to work," Chastity groans in mock dismay.

"Pfft, you love your job teaching those kids." I grin at her.

"I know, but I've spent my entire school holiday with you. I miss you." She sounds melancholy. I miss my friend too, but as I joke with her she's always on holiday so it's not like we don't get to spend time together. My argument is that we spend quality time together, whereas if she just lived round the corner then we wouldn't see each other anywhere near as much.

"Enough school talk, so when are you seeing Chris again?" She's back in interrogation mode and seems to have forgotten my previous answers as she's already asked this question a half dozen times already this morning.

"I've already told you, we don't have any plans!" I don't

know when we'll see each other, or if. I know he'd really enjoyed our night and day together because of his text, but there was no mention of anything other than he'd be in touch. Was that just a brush off? I'm not as confident with men as Chastity is, whereas she's happy to jump into bed with a different guy every week that's just not me. Mind you, neither is jumping into bed with a guy that I've only just met.

"You're thinking about him again." Chastity laughs. "You've got that dreamy 'I've been fucked very well' expression on your face again."

I punch her on the arm but we both dissolve into giggles.

"So what do you have on this week?" Is she seriously trying to ask the same question in a different way?

"Just the usual, " I reply as I pinch a handful of popcorn from the bowl she's holding rather protectively on her far side. "I've got an appointment with Jackson and the club lawyer tomorrow, but no idea why. He just said they have some paperwork they need me to sign." I shrug my shoulders.

"Ooh interesting, wonder what it could be?"

"No idea, can't be anything to do with my mother as the appointment was set up before she reappeared, but Jackson said its nothing to worry about, just dotting a few i's and crossing a few t's. You know what he's like. He keeps things close to his chest."

The theme tune to the movie blasts out from the TV and I

shush Chastity. We decided to watch Thor Ragnarok so we could ogle over Chris Hemsworth. It would be rude not to. I smile to myself watching the actor I have indecent thoughts about cross my screen, and realize just how much Chris reminds me of him. I definitely have graphic memories of my Chris! We settle back to enjoy the movie, making the most of our last day together.

CHAPTER SIXTEEN

Rebel

I'm in shock. How could Jackson not tell me what he'd had planned for all these years. He didn't even tell me on my birthday, instead he let me sit there in front of the lawyer who surprised the hell out of me. It was too much to take in. I'm still struggling to get my head around it as we sit in the coffee shop he brought me to afterwards so he could explain.

"But why?" I can't help asking.

"Because you're my daughter, in every way that counts." His smile is full of pride and love.

"But why a trust? Why now?" I just don't understand.

"I needed you to be old enough to appreciate the importance of what I've given you, to be mature enough to understand why it needs to be kept safe." I look at him, still not comprehending what's happened today. Considering the value of what he's just signed over to me I understand why he waited till my thirtieth birthday, but I still don't get why he chose me. He has family, well a sister and nieces and nephews, so why me? "You're my daughter, Rebel. You understand what it means to me, and I know you'll keep it safe."

Jackson has just signed over a huge tract of land to me, at a conservative estimate its worth a fortune to the right buyer, possibly millions. He trusts that I won't sell it, as he has no wish to see it developed and turned into a commercial monstrosity as he calls it. He goes on to explain to me that for years he's refused offers on the land from greedy developers. He'd purchased the land when he left the army, and that small investment has grown massively as the landowners around him gave in and sold out. He's held steadfast all these years and, with the help of the lawyer, placed the land in trust for me. On paper its conservatively worth a couple of hundred thousand dollars, but that's all dependent on what eventually gets built on it. Its large enough for a huge mall complex, or I could build my dream home and live there happily surrounded by nature. At the end of the day the choice is now mine, I own it. I'm with Jackson though, I can't think of anything worse than an ugly development destroying the land. Would I have said the same thing back when I was eighteen? I'd like to think I would, but I understand why he waited until now.

I've matured a lot, own my own home, have built a successful business. I'm at a point in my life where I'm comfortable. The prospect of a fortune doesn't really appeal, especially now I've met my mother. She's grown up with money and look at her, cold and heartless enough to abandon her own baby, selfish to the end. If that's what wealth does to you I don't want it.

I know the land, its where we always went camping and fishing. I have so many happy memories of spending time with Jackson there.

"It's your choice now, darlin', you can do what you want with it," he pauses, "but if you do decide to sell can you wait till I'm in the ground?"

I don't want to think about Jackson not being here, not being a part of my life. "Don't even talk like that!" I protest. "You're not allowed to die on me."

Jackson chuckles and pulls me into a hug. "That's my girl." He smiles.

"There's no rush to make a decision is there?" I ask him. "I mean I didn't even know about it until today, I'm not sure I'm ready for that responsibility." I know I can't bury my head in the sand over this, but the land has just sat there for all this time so I don't see any reason for haste.

"No, totally up to you when, and if, you want to do anything. The only thing I ask is you respect my decision not to sell to the developers whilst I'm alive, but at the end

of the day, it's your land now, so you can sell if you want."
I wish he'd stop talking about dying, he's not even old yet.
"Cheer up, Rebel." He gives me another hug. "You're a
lady of property now." He smirks.

"Well, I can't sell for a year anyway," the accountant in me
reasons. "I'd pay way too much in tax!"

"That's my girl, I knew I'd raised you right." We both
dissolve into laughter.

We chatter about inconsequential stuff whilst we drink our
coffee when I suddenly remember what I wanted to
ask him.

"So old man, at my party you were dancing with a pretty
blonde lady. Anything I should know?" I've caught him
off guard with my question and he almost chokes on the
mouthful of coffee he was drinking. Is that a blush I see
behind his beard. Wow, this must be more serious than I
thought.

"Erm, she's just a friend," he offers. I cock my head to one
side and give him my 'oh really' look. "Okay, she's a bit
more than a friend, but it's still early days." I'm pleased
for him, I love Jackson, but all the years I've known him
I've never seen him close with a woman for any length of
time. I want him to be happy and tell him so. "Thanks
darlin', you too. I just didn't want to confuse you when
you were growing up by having a string of women around
you, and I never met anyone that I thought enough of to
introduce you."

I'm slightly sad that he's been alone all these years, but at the same time I'm grateful that I never had to share him. Of all my dads' Jackson is the one that I am closest to, as well as being the one named on my adoption certificate.

"So... spill." Ah, sweet revenge. The number of times I've been on the receiving end of this conversation with him.

"Well, she's called Sue and she lives in Maldon. She runs the art store." Like a typical bloke he stops there, I roll my eyes at him and he carries on." She's a bit younger than me, she's 49 and has no kids. She's been divorced a couple of years now, it was pretty nasty, and she came here to start over as she's lost both parents and has no family." I feel sympathy for her, I can't imagine not having my family around me. I manage to draw him into telling me about a few of their dates and I like the sound of her. It's obvious that Jackson really likes her, and I hope that things work out between them.

"So when do I get to meet her?"

"You sure?" Jackson doesn't look convinced.

"Yeah, she sounds nice, and you obviously like her. It would be good to meet her, unless you're not that serious yet?" It had sounded like he was to me, but his response has me questioning myself.

"I'll set something up," he offers. "What do you fancy, coffee, meal, cinema?" I consider the options, I won't be able to chat to her properly in the cinema so that's out, and a meal might be awkward if we don't get on so suggest the coffee shop. "I'll let you know when and where." He looks relieved when I change the topic of conversation after that, bless him. I love that he feels no shame in dissecting my love life, but as soon as the tables are turned it's a different matter. I reckon I can have some fun with this.

CHAPTER SEVENTEEN

Rebel

I put the phone down on my mother and wonder why I've agreed to another coffee date. There's nothing about the woman that I like, and I don't really want to spend time in her company. I can only surmise that I'm trying to find something endearing in her character somewhere. I'm scared that this is the woman whose genes I share. Is this my future? Is this who I'm fated to become? I also know that Jackson would want me to try to forge some kind of relationship with her, because in his eyes it's the right thing to do.

I close the lid on my MacBook, unable to concentrate on the figures in front of me. I feel like my life has been turned upside down in just a few days, leaving me questioning everything I thought I knew. My whole life I've felt like something was missing, that I wasn't good enough. It wasn't the lack of a mother that bothered me, I had plenty of maternal love and guidance from my MC family. It's the whole abandonment thing. I think I managed to hide it from Jackson and my dads', at least I hope I did. I'd never want them to think that they weren't enough for me.

I suspect its why I've always struggled with men, I've always felt deep down that they'd leave me as well, so never fully invested myself in the relationship. Sighing I stand from the desk and head over to the coffee machine, popping a pod in then huffing in frustration when I hear the loud buzzing signifying its run out of water. I should have checked before I started. I can tell it's going to be one of those days. Refilling the machine from the jug of filtered water in the fridge, I finally get my cup of dark nectar. Returning to my desk I lift the lid of the MacBook and chastise myself, it's time I got down to some work. Perhaps immersing myself back in the figures will help me forget the whirlwind of thoughts that are on constant loop in my head.

I MANAGED to get through all the work I had planned for this afternoon, but don't have time to go home and change so my mother will have to deal with me turning up in my work clothes. At least they'll be more to her taste than the shorts I wore last time.

She's already seated in the coffee shop when I arrive, hidden away in a booth at the back. I wonder if she's ashamed to be seen with me? I go over and greet her, checking if she wants another drink before I go to the counter and place my own order. She greets me warmly, and I almost think she looks genuinely pleased to see me. Yeah, right. I'm imagining things. I reluctantly allow her to hug me and don't miss the wince on her face when our bodies touch. She brushes it off, telling me she's overdone it in the gym and her abs are a little tender.

"I should have listened to my trainer," she says with a chuckle. "I was trying to show off and do more than I was capable of."

That one sentence has such an impact on me, I'm not sure what happened, but I realize she's not the monster I've always thought. She's human after all. It's not enough to make up for all those years she didn't want me, but it's enough to make me decide that she does deserve a chance. It wasn't even what she said, as much as the warm way that she said it. I quickly excuse myself so I can get my coffee. I need a moment to compose myself. My emotions are all over the place at the moment, and I'm struggling to find my identity. Before my party I was happy with my life, with who I was, what I'd achieved. Now I find myself questioning everything. I'm seriously considering booking a session or two with a counsellor to help me understand what's going on with me. Normally I'd turn to Jackson and we'd talk it through, but this just feels too big and scary for that. I'm not sure he could remain impartial on this one, or that I'd take his advice if it wasn't what I wanted to hear.

I've had a lovely simple life but in the space of less than a week I've found the mother who abandoned me, or rather she found me, I've slept with a guy the first night I've met him and I've suddenly discovered I own a lot of land. I want my old simple life back.

Returning to the booth I sink into the comfortable seat opposite Deidre. "I have to say you did a fantastic job of the gala the other night." I compliment her.

"Thank you," she accepts demurely, "I had a lot of help, they did most of the work," she minimizes her involvement. "You looked stunning." She pauses a moment, "I was very proud of you."

I'm not sure how to respond to that remark, I want to shout and tell her that she has no right to be proud of anything as she means nothing to me. I bite my tongue instead, aware though of the uncomfortable silence that it leaves.

"Thank you, it was a beautiful gown wasn't it?" I offer her an olive branch.

We chat a little about the shop where I purchased the gown, and she recommends another store that I might like to try. This is safe conversation, I can handle this, although I'm not sure I'll have reason to purchase another gown and tell her so.

"I only went because the cause was so close to my heart. I've always had an affinity for abandoned children." I want to bite back the words as soon as they leave my mouth, they weren't said harshly or with cruel intention but it's obvious from the pain on Deidre's face that they hurt. "I'm sorry, I didn't mean anything by that!" I rush to apologize.

"It's okay," she brushes the hurtful comment away. "I'd have understood if you had." She reaches across the table and takes my hand in hers. "What I did was wrong, but believe me, at the time I really believed it was the best thing for you. Whatever you may think of me, please know that what I did, I did for you and not from any selfish desire on my own part." She pauses a moment, as if considering what she's going to say next. "I still think it was the best thing, the safest thing." As though realizing she's revealed too much she changes the conversation suddenly, asking me how I know Chris.

"I met him at the gala, why, do you know him?" I'm confused, Chris never intimated he knew Deidre, but then I don't think she ever came up as a topic of conversation.

"He works for my husband," she reveals. "You looked to be getting on very well?"

"I like him, I think he likes me, but I haven't heard from him since." I reply. Unconsciously I check the screen on my phone, as I have been doing frequently since he dropped me off at home. There's still no message from him.

Deidre chuckles quietly having caught me checking my phone. "I think perhaps it's a little more than like," she smiles at me "My advice is just take it nice and slow, a man needs to think he's in control."

I cannot believe I'm sat here talking to my mother about a guy. This is so surreal and so unexpected. With a slight shock, I realize that I'm actually quite enjoying her company. Yep, my life sure has changed this last week. The best I can do is just embrace it and go with it.

CHAPTER EIGHTEEN

Deidre

I hate my life. I hate what I'm being asked to do. I'm surrounded by all of this hate, but my heart is full of love. Love for the daughter that I abandoned all those years ago. I promised myself I wouldn't get attached. I failed, I failed so hard. That first meeting at the country club had been awkward and strained, but today in the coffee shop I saw the real Rebel, and my heart burst with love and pride. She's an amazing young woman, and I really enjoyed the time we spent together. I think she did too.

I wish I could keep her safe, that Robert didn't see her as the only solution to his predicament. Knowing Robert as well as I do, there can be no happy ending here. He'll use her, then destroy her. I can't think of any way out of this. If I thought for one minute that killing Robert would keep her safe, I'd do it. I'd gladly sacrifice my life to save hers, but Robert owes money to some pretty unsavory characters and I'm not sure that debt would die with him. They want what Rebel has. They won't give up until they get it.

I can tell from our conversation that she likes Chris, I wonder how he feels about her. Can he really just see her as a work task? She's so warm and open I hope that she'll have won him over with her charms, but she said he hadn't been back in touch. I'm surprised as Robert had been very insistent that Chris got her on side. I think Chris is a good guy deep down, I know he hates Robert, but at the end of the day he loves his mother and he's doing all of this to keep her safe and to keep her treatment funded. How far would he go, how low would he stoop? He's Roberts flesh and blood so there's every chance he shares some of his father's evil. As much as I want to believe that nurture beats nature, I can't be sure. I want to talk to him, find out where his true loyalties lie, yet am reluctant to do so in case he runs straight back to Robert and betrays me.

I've never felt as helpless and alone as I do today. I have no one to turn to, confide in or ask for support. My father and Robert have made sure of that. The mask I've worn all these years has been too effective, I've isolated myself from anyone who might have wanted to care. Society has so many rules and expectations that have made that easy. I envy Rebel her freedom, her care free life. The only time I managed to experience anything resembling happiness were those few months of rebellion before I became pregnant. How I wish I'd run away, changed my name and lived my own life. Even back then I knew it couldn't happen, I wasn't naive enough to believe my father wouldn't track me down. I've paid every day since, condemned to a life of abuse from Robert. It's a good job he didn't want to be a father as his constant abuse of my body meant I couldn't have another child. I know my father was disappointed I didn't give him a grandson, but I'm relieved. I could never condemn a child to this life. I suspect that Robert has fathered more than one child with his string of mistresses, although to my knowledge he's never acknowledged any of them. He's too narcissistic to share the limelight with anyone, even a child. He demands attention like a needy toddler, always taking, taking and never giving anything in return.

I try and come up with options. I could come clean, tell Rebel everything and beg her to comply with Roberts demands, but why would she. She owes no loyalty to me. I could ask Chris for help, but I'm not confident he would risk his mother's care. She's never been there for me, never once shown that she cared. I often wonder if she feels as trapped in her life as I do. I hoped that when my father died I'd see a different side to her, that the release from his constraints would help her become the mother she should have been. She's still as cold and heartless as ever.

There is nowhere to turn. No one who can help. I'm stuck on this path. I stop my frustrated pacing and sink to the floor, finally letting the tears flow freely. The tears aren't for me, I know my fate and accept it, they're for my baby girl. The baby girl I cannot save. The baby girl I love more than ever.

Rebel

The ding of my phone pulls me from the bank reconciliation I was working on. I glance over half-heartedly, still trying to work out the error I know is in front of me. The text alert sits on the phone screen showing an unknown number. I almost ignore it and go back to the statement but something makes me swipe it open. I let out a squeal of joy when I realize it's from Chris, and that he does want to see me again. I'd convinced myself it was a one off after several days of his silence.

Unknown Number: Hi, sorry I've not been in touch, I've been out of state on business. I really enjoyed our time together and hope that you did too. Do you feel like getting together one night this week?

I consider my response, remembering what my mother said about taking things slowly. As much as I want to reply immediately with a huge HELL YES! I take note of her advice. I put the phone to one side and go back to the statement. Let him sweat a bit. It won't do any harm. I grin when I spot the error the hotel book keeper has made, she's transposed the figures. I make a quick correction and take satisfaction from the zero figure that appears once the two columns balance as they should. Why can't life be simple as figures? I spend another hour finishing up my work on the hotel books before I consider replying to Chris's text.

Rebel: I enjoyed our time together too. I'm quite busy this week but could meet up Friday night if that's convenient?

You big fat liar, I laugh at my reply. I have absolutely nothing on this week but I'm not telling him that. The most exciting thing I'm likely to have on outside of work is a movie night with a tub of Ben and Jerry's for company. My phone dings with a reply almost instantly.

Unknown number: Sounds good, I'll pick you up at seven from yours. Wear something casual x

I smile to myself and save his number to the contacts on my phone. I'm looking forward to my date already, and wish it was sooner. It feels like forever between now and Friday, but I'm sure it will pass quickly enough. With that in mind I busy myself with booking in to the hairdressers and the beauticians. I might as well make sure that I look my best. Mentally running through my wardrobe I think I should treat myself to some new lingerie, just in case! He's said to wear something casual and I've no idea what that means. Shutting down my MacBook I decide that some retail therapy is called for and head off to see if I can find any inspiration. Roll on Friday!

CHAPTER NINETEEN

Deidre

Rebel looks beautiful today, her face is glowing and she's full of happiness. How I envy her that. I'm excited that she invited me this time, suggesting we get together. Even though this was her choice, it breaks my heart. No good can come of a relationship between us. It's only a couple of days since we last saw each other, and I can feel a bond starting to form. I need to move slowly, regardless of what Robert wants. I have to gain her trust, forge a relationship where she'll be comfortable enough to listen to any advice I offer. That doesn't happen overnight. He's so used to getting what he wants that he has no idea how the real world works. He thinks he can snap his fingers and just like that the whole plan will be accomplished. He's a fool, but he's bloody dangerous with it. I'm walking a fine line here, trying to ensure my daughters safety without losing my connection with her.

I'm scared that when she realizes what he's after she'll want nothing to do with me. She'll think that the only reason I got in touch with her was to accomplish the task and she won't believe that I've never stopped thinking about her, never stopped loving her. Who could blame her.

"I've got a date with Chris on Friday," she confesses, "I was hoping you'd come shopping with me, help me choose an outfit?"

"That's wonderful news." I hope my face doesn't show what I'm really feeling. I'm scared of Chris getting close to her, I don't know if he's doing this because he genuinely likes her, or just because Robert told him to. I can't bear to see Chris break her heart if it's not real. "I'm not sure we share the same dress style though." My laugh sounds false to my ears, luckily she doesn't notice.

"He's told me to dress casually, and I guess that you have more idea of what he means by that than I do."

"Where's he taking you?"

"I've no idea," she smiles dreamily. "Just that he's picking me up at seven and I have to wear casual dress." I can tell she's excited about her date.

"Well I think we should go safe with jeans and a smart shirt," I suggest. "Simple but stylish." Rebel nods her head in agreement.

We spend a little time chatting about her childhood while we're enjoying our coffee. I can tell that she's had a life full of love and I can't begin to imagine what that would be like. She seems to be really close to her family, even if it's not a standard family unit set up. Who am I to judge? I came from a supposedly perfect family and yet I've always felt alone. It's true what they say, you can choose your friends but you can't choose your relatives. I try to discourage her questions about my upbringing, and encourage her to do all the talking. It's obvious by the way that she talks about him that Jackson has been her primary carer, and am a little shocked that they chose not to do a DNA test to establish paternity. If I'm honest I really didn't expect them to keep her, I thought they'd hand her over to the state and she'd be adopted by some well to do couple and lead a normal life. Regardless of the unconventional way that she has been raised, she's turned into a good person, she's intelligent and hardworking and very caring. A daughter that any mother would be proud of and I tell her so. She blushes at the compliment, she's also very humble.

I'm surprised she hasn't expressed shock that I don't actually know who her father is, just that he was a member of the club. How do I explain to her what I was feeling at that time? How innocent I was, yet desperate to rebel against such a strict patriarch.

"I was a virgin you know, when I went to that first party," I confess. Rebel's eyes widen at my admission.

"But you were in your early twenties weren't you?"

"I'd just celebrated my twenty-first birthday when my

parents went to Europe. I'd been brought up in a very sheltered household. My father had ambitions for me and hadn't found the right partner for me to marry." I shrug my shoulders.

"Your father was finding your husband for you?" She sounds shocked, I suppose anyone brought up in a normal home would be.

"From an early age I always knew that I would have my husband chosen for me, I mean I barely had any control over my wardrobe so something as important as my future life partner couldn't be left to me." Rebel is shaking her head in shock.

"But why?"

"My father had high political ambitions, he never wanted a daughter, he wanted a son who would be a rising star in politics and then eventually become Prime Minister. Instead, he got me. Back then it wasn't acceptable for a woman to be interested in politics so I had to marry the right man, someone who would be suitable to fulfill my father's dreams." I have to laugh at the mistake he made in choosing Robert, the guy has gambled so much there's no way he could attain a position as anything other than a local councilor. There's too much dirt in his background. Rebel is looking at me curiously and I realize I must have laughed out loud. I need to be careful what I tell her about Robert, too much too soon and I could scare her off. "There were a few candidates he thought might be suitable, but their parents had already made other alliances for them. Finding the right man took time, and of course I had to be a virgin on my wedding night."

"I can't believe that kind of thing happened," she looks appalled.

"It's the world I grew up in, I knew it was what was expected of me." I shrug my shoulders and sigh.

"But what about love?" Rebel's face is so earnest, she's so lucky that she believes in 'The One' and 'Happy Ever After'. They were never an option for me.

"Love is frivolous, a good marriage is more important." I flatly repeat my Mother's words, I learned them by rote. "It's how I was raised." I try to explain. Looking at Rebel I don't think there's any way for her to understand my life, she's been raised enjoying free will and allowed to have her own voice and opinions. "It's one of the reasons I gave you away," I reach for her hand. "I didn't want you being forced to live the life I was destined for."

"Have you ever loved anyone?" Rebel's question throws me.

"I've never been loved," I answer instead, it's easier to say those words than to answer what she's asked. I lift my coffee cup even though it's empty, I'm just trying to distract myself now.

"Not even by your parents?" Her voice is full of shock.

"No, I was an accessory, nothing more." I sigh.

"But that's so wrong!" Rebel exclaims, there's a hint of

anger in her tone now. She's definitely a supporter of lost causes bless her.

"But, have you ever loved anyone?" She repeats.

"Just one person," I look her straight in the eye as I respond. "My daughter."

CHAPTER TWENTY

Rebel

I'm blown away by my mother's confession in the coffee shop. As we stroll around the mall I keep turning and looking at her. I gasp when I realize I thought of her as my mother and not Deidre. When did that change? I'm sure there's a lot that she's holding back, but she's shown me a part of herself today that I never expected. From what she shared, my mother didn't abandon me because she didn't want me. She truly thought that by leaving me at those gates, she was giving me a better life, even if that life didn't include her. I'm not sure I can get my head around this. For as long as I can remember I've hated the woman. Perhaps hate is too strong a word, but there certainly hasn't been any interest in knowing who she was or meeting her. From all outward appearances she's the epitome of society, but I can see beneath the surface there's a different woman. There's a woman who yearns for fun and adventure, and most sad of all, a woman who has never experienced love. How can you go through life and never know what love is? It's so unfair.

From our conversation it sounds like the closest thing she had to affection was a series of nannies, although none ever lasted any significant length of time. Even in the books I read where a hot billionaire has been raised by a nanny they've been there for his whole life, they're the ones who've shown him what love is. I think if I had read my mother's life in a book or saw it in a movie I'd say it was too far-fetched to be true, especially in this day and age.

She talks about her life as though she doesn't matter. She's only just over fifty, she's not old enough to be talking as though her life is over. She's got years ahead of her. I need to help ensure that those years are drastically different to her past, and to try and make her present a lot more enjoyable as well.

I'm distracted by a pair of heels in a shop window when I hear my mother squeal just before she grabs my arm. I'm dragged into a store before I have chance to work out what it sells and blush to my roots when I see she's pulled me into a high end lingerie boutique.

"You need something extra special for your date on Friday," she says with a huge grin on her face.

"I am not buying lingerie with my mother." I laugh.

"Pfft. You're right, you're not buying it. I am." She chuckles, ignoring my protestations and pulling me to a rack of the most beautiful lingerie I've ever seen. I gasp when I spot the price tag on the tiny pair of knickers in my eye line. There's no way I could justify that price for that! There's barely any material on it. "Don't even think about it," she warns as she sees my shocked expression as I finger the price tag. "This is my treat."

My mother selects several sets for me and encourages me to make my own choices as well. Thankfully, she doesn't follow me into the changing room. I'm not that comfortable with her yet that I could let her see me naked. I have to admit as much as I like the selections I made, her choices are much more flattering. They're sexy without being trashy and I feel like a million dollars in them. I settle on a soft white set that enhances my heavy bust without making it look any bigger than it already is. Thankfully neither of us chose any thongs as I can't stand the thought of that tiny slip of fabric between my ass cheeks.

When I head out she's waiting for me, sat there sipping on a glass of champagne. I chuckle, this is definitely not the kind of store I'd normally frequent. "All done?" She tilts her head to indicate the lingerie in my hands.

"Yep, they all look great, but this is the one." I hold up the white set she chose and she smiles in approval.

"They all fit though?"

"Yep, they all looked great, but there was something about

this set." The assistant reaches out her hand and I pass her the items I've discarded and turn to head for the cash register, slightly unsure where it is in the store. I'm confused when she reaches for the white set as well. "Oh no, this is the set I'm keeping." I smile at her. The assistant just grins and takes them anyway, disappearing off into a corner of the store. "What the heck?" I call after her. "I wanted that set!"

My mother finishes the glass in her hand and chuckles at my obvious ire. "Don't worry about it, come on." She guides me so that we're following the path the assistant had taken. When we reach the register there's a bag ready and waiting for me, full of tissue paper and beautifully wrapped with ribbons. My mother pulls her credit card from her purse and it's only then that I register the amount, it's over a $1000 and I try and stop her. The assistant obviously made a mistake.

"No dear, I told her if they all fit that we'd buy them all." She grins at me. The assistant behind the counter smirks at me, and I have to bite my tongue. There's a part of me that would love to reach out and slap the smile from her face. Instead, I accept the package she hands me with good grace and thank her as we leave.

"You shouldn't have." I hiss quietly at my mother as we leave the store.

"Oh shut up," she grins back at me. "That was fun!"

The rest of the shopping trip is the same. She chooses the stores and I just play mannequin, trying on the selection she's made for me, and a few of my own if I find something I like. If it fits then she buys it. I'm not sure my wardrobe is big enough to handle all these purchases, and every time I tried to protest I was shushed. When I tried not taking in any outfits I'd chosen she just handed me more of hers. I couldn't win.

My feet are sore by the time we've finished selecting the right outfit for my date on Friday and I gladly accept her suggestion of dinner in the small Italian bistro. I love Italian food and I really need to sit down.

The waiter is charming and spends most of the meal flattering my mother, who plays along beautifully, even chatting back to him in Italian. I have no idea what they're saying but I can't help smiling as I'm sure from their expressions they're flirting with each other.

The meal passes quickly, and I'm surprised by how comfortable I feel in my mother's company. It's odd but it feels like I've known her forever already, and I realize that I actually like her, a lot. When you dig beneath the society exterior, there's a really nice person below. There's still something about her that I can't quite put my finger on. When she doesn't think I'm looking, there's definitely a haunted expression in her eyes. It's more than her regretting the years we have lost. I raise my glass in a toast to my mother, and silently vow to myself that I will find out what it is that's bothering her and help to put it right.

CHAPTER TWENTY-ONE

Rebel

I really enjoyed spending time with my mother, but I have to say it's always nice to come home. I sink gratefully into the sofa, having kicked my shoes off at the door, then poured a glass of wine. I glance at the post in my hand and discard most of it as generic, bills and circulars. One official looking letter stands out. It's on legal sized paper and I don't recognize the name of the corporation that has sent it. I use my nail to open the thick envelope, tutting when it takes several attempts and shreds of white paper fall away. I hate mess. I gather the scraps from the flap of the envelope and put them on the sofa arm beside me. Drawing out the heavy documents I'm still none the wiser.

What the fuck? Who even knows I own the land? I only

found out myself yesterday and already some faceless corporation is trying to get me to sell. My eyes widen when I see the amount they're offering, $475,000 isn't to be sniffed at, but I disregard it immediately. Like I told Jackson, even if I was to sell I'd wait a year as I've no desire to pay over the odds in tax. As it is I've no desire to ever sell, anyway. I scrunch the thick papers into a ball without reading them further. I'm so angry I toss them across the room, missing the waste bin and knocking over a photo of me and Chastity taken at the clubhouse last summer. I huff my way over the room to retrieve the trash, setting the picture frame straight again before I head into the kitchen to discard the rubbish properly.

I didn't read it all so I've no idea if they were expecting a reply, but they're not getting one. The bloody cheek. I take a large gulp of wine but it doesn't calm my nerves. I pace angrily around my small living room, my lovely mood from earlier decimated by the intrusion of the greedy developers into my sanctuary. I feel soiled. I know it's stupid and it's nothing more than words on paper, but that's how I feel.

I debate calling Jackson, but I guess he did warn me that this would happen. I just hadn't expected it to happen so soon. Instead I call my friend Chastity, she's only been gone a few days but I miss her.

"Yo, bitch, wassup?" She greets me warmly in typical Chastity fashion. I feel better already just hearing her voice.

"I went shopping with my mother and I have a date on Friday night." I offer.

"What the fuck? You went shopping with your mother? You're calling her mother?" Chastity is practically screeching down the phone at me. "What the hell did I miss? Did you bang your head or something?" She chuckles.

I can see why she's so surprised. I'm shocked by how quickly a bond is forming, considering my previous beliefs. "I can't explain it, but she's definitely not the woman I thought she was." I sigh and tell Chastity about our shopping trip and meal. "She said something earlier that really changed how I think though." I go on to explain about my mother having never felt she was loved.

Chastity gasps down the phone. "That's so sad." She's been raised in a house full of love as well, and I know she too will be struggling to understand how a parent can fail to show their child love. We spend a little longer discussing the pros and cons of arranged marriages, it's not something either of us agrees with or feels comfortable with. We're both far too independent to understand a woman wanting to participate in one. "I suppose though, with my dating history maybe my mom would have made a better choice than me." Chastity giggles. She's definitely had more partners than I have, but she's always seemed happy to 'love em and leave em' as she calls it.

"Have you heard from George yet?" I ask.

"Who the hell is George?" I can hear the confusion in her voice, and can picture her shaking her head on the other end of the phone.

"The guy who took you home from the gala." I inform her.

"Oh, him, na." She doesn't seem bothered. I'd thought they were getting on well, I must have been wrong.

"Thought you liked him?"

"He was okay," she mumbles, flooring me with her next comment. "You were so into Chris, and I knew you wouldn't go for it with me having called dibs so I hooked up with George to let you off the hook."

"What?" I can't keep the shock out of my voice.

"You two seemed made for each other, it's no big deal." She replies. "Hang on, did you say earlier you had a date on Friday?" She's swiftly changed the topic on me. I'll let her get away with it this time, but make a mental note to re-visit the George situation.

We're on the phone a good hour, dissecting each other's lives, gossiping about friends and planning my outfit for Friday now I have so many new clothes to choose from. She persuades me to try a few of them on and send her selfies so she can give her opinion. We eventually decide on some skinny black jeans that make my ass and legs look great and pair it with a cream silk blouse with an open collar and long sleeves. As I'm still not sure where we're going we can't decide whether to pair it with my black leather knee high boots, my black heels or my low black pumps.

"You might even need to wear your Vans hon'," Chastity advises. She's right. I'll have to have them all ready by the door and see where we're going before I can decide.

"Are you excited about Friday?" Chastity asks.

"Yeah, it's weird as we've already slept together so it shouldn't feel so awkward, but I get butterflies every time I think about it," I confess.

"Aw that's so sweet." Chastity laughs, I know she's taking the piss out of me and tell her so. "But you know you love me really." She's right, I love her like a sister and that's the only reason she's getting away with this.

"I love you, but you're pushing your luck." I laugh back.

We end the call with me promising to ring her with an update on Saturday, where no doubt she'll dissect my date moment by moment and want all the salacious details. She can want. Some things aren't meant for sharing. I'm not sure there'll be any salacious details to share, I've only had that one text from him since he dropped me off. It might just have been a drunken one off. I hope not, but only time will tell.

I take my empty wine glass into the kitchen, washing and drying it so I can put it away and keep the worktops clear. As I pull the blind down on the window above the sink I could swear I saw a movement in the garden, but after standing there a while I see nothing else so put it down to my imagination. I go round the house ensuring the doors and windows are locked before heading to my bathroom and drawing a bubble bath. My feet are aching after our shopping escapade and a long hot soak before bed will do me the world of good.

CHAPTER TWENTY-TWO

Rebel

F riday afternoon has dragged. As tempted as I am to leave early I have work to do, and it's not fair on my clients not to give them my full attention. Today the columns of figures aren't soothing me like they normally do, they're frustrating the hell out of me because I'm impatient for this evening to arrive.

My phone dings with a text from my mother, and it brings a smile to my face to know that she is thinking of me.

Hope you have a great time tonight, love you, Mom x

Mom. I roll the word around on my tongue and I like the feel of it, the sound of it. I open her contact details on my phone and edit them to show the caller ID as Mom. It just seems right. I don't have a photo of her that I can add, I'll have to get one of us together the next time we meet up.

The text from my Mom has made the afternoon a lot brighter, allowing me to return to work minus my earlier frustration. I look at the spreadsheet in front of me with fresh enthusiasm and lose myself in figures until it's time to head home.

I'M NERVOUSLY PACING my living room, he's not due for another ten minutes but I wanted to make sure I was ready in plenty of time. I feel like I'm wearing a hole in the carpet as I tread back and forth. I have my Vans on, but the other footwear sits waiting by the door for me. I wonder where he's taking me, but can't guess. I know so little about him, other than how his body feels against mine. I don't know much about his family, other than he has a mother in a nursing home. We didn't talk about anything in any depth at the gala dinner, and I've probably forgotten most of what was said thanks to those bloody shots that knocked me out.

I'm lost in memories of us in bed together when a truck pulls into the yard, pulling me from my happy thoughts. I'm so bloody nervous, I feel more like a teenage girl than a thirty year old woman. I open the door and feel like swooning. He looks so hot. It's as if a mix of all my fantasies are rolled into one and standing there on my porch. Without realizing it I lick my lips and Chris just smirks at me.

"You ready?" His eyes trail up and down my body giving me an approving look before he leans in and kisses me on the cheek. It's such as sweet greeting, stealing just a little more of my heart than he had before.

"Yeah, I just need to grab my purse. I wasn't sure what shoes to wear though." I glance at my feet.

"They're perfect." He smiles at me. I grab my purse from the back of the sofa and accept the arm he offers me as he watches me lock up before guiding me to his car. "Nice house," he offers once we're seated.

"It's not much but it's mine, and I love it." I grin back at him. "So, where are we heading?" I ask him.

"It's a surprise." He's amused by the huffy expression on my face, but refuses to give in to my interrogation. "Patience is a virtue."

"It's also a virtue I have never possessed." I laugh out in response. We talk about inconsequential things on the short drive, the weather, the TV show we both watched last night and the music that's playing on the local radio station throughout the journey. By the time we pull up outside the bowling alley I've relaxed and I feel totally comfortable in his company. I look at the bowling alley in horror when we're parked up. "Really?" I whisper. "I haven't been bowling in years." I was never that good when I went regularly as a teenager, with all those years of absence I dread to think how bad my game will be.

"You'll be fine," Chris reassures me. "You'll soon remember what to do."

The interior has had a refit since I was last here and looks more modern and inviting. The aroma of stale grease has been replaced with one of appetizing food and the carpet is no longer sticking to my feet. Because it's a Friday night they're doing a bowling and burger deal accompanied by disco lighting and loud music. It's so far removed from what I'd expected, but I like it. It's certainly more me than a fancy French restaurant that's for sure.

I place my Vans on the counter and eye the heavy bowling shoes with distaste. They're the most unflattering shoes I've ever worn, and my feet feel cold as I place them inside. I guess the only good thing is that everyone in here is wearing them. Chris checks the numbers above the lanes and guides me to lane one at the far side of the building. He gestures to the console and lets me enter our names. It's not long before he bellows with laughter when he sees the name Thor appear on the monitor. He doesn't look surprised when I enter my name as Sif. "So you're my wife now are you?" He laughs.

"I didn't realize you knew Norse mythology," I compliment him.

"I half expected you to put Jane, from the first two movies." He tips me a nod, acknowledging my play.

Chris is first to bowl and I groan when he scores a strike with his first ball. This is going to be a long night I think, and am proved right when my first ball rolls down the gutter from the midway point, no intention of going anywhere near the pins. Chris rolls his eyes at my pathetic performance, but hands me a slightly heavier weight ball and gives me a few tips on my posture. Taking note of his suggestions I look straight ahead, visualizing the pins in front of me. I put everything I have behind the ball and shriek in joy as it hits its target and pins scatter, then groan when I realize there are two pins left standing, one either side of the lane.

"Not bad," he compliments me with a kiss on my forehead. The first game passes in a riot of laughter and cheating. It's only fair to point out that all the cheating was on my side as I tried to distract him whenever it was his turn. He took it in his stride, continuing to support me with advice, whilst he hits a strike almost every turn. At the end of the first game I have a reasonable score for me, but I'm miles behind Chris. The waitress saves any further embarrassment for me when she shows up with our food and a couple of soda's. Beer was an option but I want a clear head tonight, I don't want to forget a moment of our time together, unlike last time.

I'm sure Chris doesn't try as hard in the second game as his score is lower, and with his help mine has risen. I'm still the loser, but I've had a really good evening. My chest aches from all the laughter, and my lips are swollen from the kisses we shared. The lane beside us was empty the whole time and it's was like we were in our own little paradise.

The drive back to mine seems such an anti-climax after the

fun night that we've shared. I'm not sure what is coming next, what Chris's expectations are if any. This evening was such a classic first date.

We pull up on my driveway and Chris turns to me, damn this looks like goodnight. Disappointment floods my body, but is soon replaced by heat when he asks if it's not too presumptuous of him to come in for a coffee.

"Absolutely not." I grin back at him.

The front door has barely shut before I'm pulled into his arms. All thoughts of coffee are forgotten as I lead him into my bedroom, clothes discarded behind us as we go.

"Hope you're not tired." Chris kisses his way down my neck.

"Not at all," I reply, satisfied by the groan I receive as my greedy hands find my goal inside his boxers. "I think it's time for dessert now, don't you."

"I'm so pleased to hear that." His reply is hoarse with lust, which is replaced by soft moans of satisfaction as I fall to my knees in front of him.

CHAPTER TWENTY-THREE

Rebel

I wake up and sense there is something different in my room. I'm still dazed with sleep and it takes me a moment to realize what it is. I'm not alone in my bed. I've never shared my bed in this room with anyone. I roll over and see the most amazing view. Chris is still asleep, he looks so relaxed and at peace. He should be, we spent a long time last night exercising this mattress, I can still feel the amazing afterglow. I lie there watching him, happy and content in the moment. My bladder is complaining and is probably what woke me, but it can wait. I'm cherishing the view. Chris must sense me watching him although I'm not sure how. He opens his eyes and grins at me.

"Mornin' beautiful." He moves his head a little closer and greets me with a soft kiss. My ovaries are exploding. I cannot get enough of this man, and still can't believe he chose me.

"Morning." I smile in return then realize I haven't brushed my teeth yet. "I'll be right back!" I screech, dashing for the en-suite. I didn't lock the door behind me, I've never had reason living here alone, so am surprised when Chris comes in as I'm brushing my teeth. Thank god he didn't come in whilst I was on the toilet. He walks up behind me and wraps his arms around me. His chest feels hot against my back, and my skin heats as he trails gentle kisses along my neck, all the while I'm brushing my teeth. I look at his reflection in the mirror in front of us and roll my eyes at him.

"Really?" I splutter with a mouth full of toothpaste. "You couldn't wait?"

"Nope, I needed to say good morning to my girl." No sooner have I rinsed the mouthwash down the sink than he's turned me round and pulled me in, placing a kiss on the end of my nose. I'm out of my depth here, I don't do sleepovers, I barely do men. I'm not sure what the correct protocol is. I decide to throw caution to the wind and kiss him back. The light kiss turns into something deeper, tongues fighting tongues, and hands exploring each other's bodies.

"What do you want for breakfast?" I finally pull away and ask him breathlessly.

"You," he says it so softly, but with so much emotion, it stops me in my tracks. Not for long though as he scoops me up into his arms and carries me back into the bedroom. He throws me back onto the bed, caging my body beneath his own. I look up at him and giggle. "What the hell?" I've broken the moment and he sounds confused.

"I'm sorry," I can't stop giggling. "But if this was a movie how cheesy would this be?" I laugh out.

"Cheesy?" He sounds disgruntled. "Darlin', this is anything but cheesy. Let me show you," he offers.

Chris does show me, and he's right. It's not cheesy, it's hot as hell. Breakfast is forgotten and it's lunchtime before we surface, reminded by the grumbling of his stomach. This is how every morning should start. Reluctantly I leave the warmth of the bed and head into the kitchen to make food for my man. My man. I like the sound of that.

THE POST IS UNOPENED on the counter where I threw it when I started lunch. Chris notices it and picks up the heavy white envelope that looks remarkably familiar. "What's this, looks official?" He asks with interest.

"It's just junk mail." I dismiss it with a nod of my head and walk over to the table to place the food I've just prepared.

"Really? Posh looking junk mail." He follows me to the table and takes a seat, dropping the envelope at the side of his plate.

I try to ignore the letter, but can't help glancing at it every few minutes whilst I try and eat. It's putting me off my lunch. I've made bacon and egg sandwiches, and the bread is forming a lump in my throat every time I try and swallow whenever I think of the letter. I guess I'll have to formally decline their offer for the land, or they'll continue to harass me. Chris is watching me, he's curious but I'm not going to let it spoil our day together. I'll try and ignore it and hope he doesn't bring the subject back up. I haven't even told Jackson about it yet so don't feel comfortable discussing private stuff with an outsider. I smile at the memories of the evening and morning we shared together and guess that makes Chris more than just an outsider. He sees my smile and gives me a knowing look.

"Thinking impure thoughts again?" He smirks.

"Me? I couldn't possibly. I'm a good girl." I mock protest.

Chris bellows with laughter. "Oh you were very good alright," he chuckles. "Although I think my definition of good and yours may be slightly different."

I feel a blush heating my cheeks. He's right though, it was very good. "Well, I suggest that you shut up and eat your lunch if you ever want a repeat," I reply brazenly. I'm so not used to this kind of sexual banter, or even the chemistry that I feel between Chris and me.

"Yes miss." He grins, picking up his sandwich to continue his meal.

Once the meal is finished Chris stands beside me at the sink, drying the pots as I wash them. This feels comfortable and natural, and not what I would have expected. Hopefully he's forgotten about the letter which is still sitting on the kitchen table.

"So what do you want to do this afternoon?" He asks.

I'm a little taken aback that he wants to continue spending his day with me, I'd kind of expected him to dash off once lunch was over. I'm secretly pleased that he hasn't rushed off. "Not sure, what do you want to do?"

Chris gives me a leer and I laugh.

"No, my hoo ha needs a breather! Think of something outside of the bedroom."

His face falls but his eyes are still full of laughter. "Yeah, I kind of need a rest and recoup." He smirks. "What about a walk?"

It's a gorgeous day outside and I think it's a great suggestion.

"I know just the place," I suggest. He raises an eyebrow at me. "It's a surprise."

"Oooh I like surprises," he replies. "Especially if you end up naked at the end of it."

"Shush, you've a one track mind." I laugh. "Give me fifteen and I'll be ready to go." I've piqued his curiosity now, but he's a good boy and waits patiently whilst I busy myself packing a cooler and finding a blanket. His eyes raise again when he sees that being packed. "It's not that kind of walk," I remind him.

As we pull away in my Kia I question what I'm doing. Am I ready to take Chris here? There are so many good memories associated with the land that Jackson has signed over to me, and I can't think of a better place to go for a walk. There's a creek there that I love and I plan on putting the blanket down and having a mini picnic, although I'm not against a little smooching if it happens.

I take the unmarked side road and watch Chris from the side of my eye. From the outside you'd never know this place was here. The road is a heavy dirt track, but suitable for vehicles. At the end, the dry land turns into an oasis of green along the creek. It looks stunning. The tall trees provide shade, the creek soothes with its bubbling soundtrack and it's so quiet that you feel like you're in the middle of nowhere, just the two of you. There's no way I can sell this place.

CHAPTER TWENTY-FOUR

Rebel

Why do weekends fly by so quickly? I swear they go at twice the speed of a weekday. Chris stayed over Saturday night and well into Sunday morning before he got called back into work. He looked so reluctant to go that I felt sorry for him. I hated waving goodbye as his truck pulled away, but busied myself in the housework I'd normally have done Saturday morning. I've never had so much sex, so it's probably a good thing for my hoo ha that he left. I strongly suspect anymore would have broken it! I grin at the memory.

My office looks so humdrum today, and I'm not in the mood for work, but needs must. Before I start though, I need to respond to the official letter about the land sale. I need to email them and tell them it's not going to happen so they'll stop hassling me. I did consider a formal written letter, but there's an email address under their letterhead and it's a lot easier to just drop a few lines.

Once the email is sent, I switch back into accountant mode, losing myself in the figures until lunchtime. It's only the grumbling of my stomach that alerts me to the time. I've not even stopped for a refill of coffee. I need to put that right immediately. I curse lightly when I realize I've run out of coffee pods, but that's okay, I can call at the store on my way home for the pods and I'll grab a sandwich and an americano from the bistro instead. I'll eat at my desk as I need to get as much done as I can, I'm not working late tonight as Jackson is finally introducing me to Sue after work.

I feel a flutter of nervousness, she obviously means a lot to him and I'm honored that he wants me to meet her. I hope she likes me. She seems to be important to him and I don't want to do anything that would get in the way of that. The bistro is busy and I have a short wait, that's okay, the coffee is worth it. The queue is small and I'm surprised when I feel the customer behind me bump into me. I turn round and see a familiar face, although I can't quite place it.

"Hello, I'm so sorry about that." The man apologizes. "I'm George," he introduces himself. "We met at the gala the other week, I escorted your charming friend home."

That's where I know him from. "Hi, nice to see you again." I smile in response.

"So what are you doing in here?" He indicates the bistro.

"Just grabbing lunch and a coffee to go, my office is just around the corner."

"You're not stopping?" He sounds disappointed. "I was hoping you'd sit with me, I have a half hour to kill before my next meeting and I hate eating alone."

I want to say that I really don't have the time today, but the look on his face is so forlorn I decide to give him the half hour. "I guess I could spare the time," I agree reluctantly. It's not like I really know the guy, but a break from my desk won't do me any harm.

George insists on paying for lunch and I politely accept. Lunch is full of stilted small talk. He's polite and pleasant enough, but I'm not sure he's very sincere. There's just something about him that seems a little off. He asks about Chastity and I'm careful with my responses. I don't want to get in the way of something for my friend, but my instinct tells me this isn't a guy she would be into. He seems very straight laced and that is most definitely not her type.

I'm relieved when I check my watch and see enough time has passed for me to make a polite exit.

"Thank you for having lunch with me, I hope we'll bump into each other again." He shakes my hand as I stand to leave the table. Silently I hope we don't. It's not an experience I'm in a rush to repeat.

THANKS to my unexpected lunch I'm later leaving the office than I wanted to be. I hate rushing and am flustered as I push open the door of the bistro. I'd wanted to make a good impression on Sue, but haven't even had time to tame my wavy locks never mind apply a coat of lipstick. She's going to get the messy Rebel I'm afraid.

Jackson and Sue are already seated when I get there, but both greet me with warm smiles, even Sue gives me a hug.

"I've been so scared about meeting you," she confesses.

"Me too!" I answer. We both laugh out loud and there's an instant bond between us. I feel comfortable in her presence, a far cry from my earlier experience with George.

There's a familiarity between Jackson and Sue that tells me they've been a couple for a while now. I'm slightly hurt that Jackson has kept this hidden from me, and guilty at the same time that he felt he needed to. He's sacrificed such a huge part of his life for me. I'm glad he's finally allowed himself to be happy. Apparently, my party was the first time Sue had been to the clubhouse, and she still hasn't properly met everyone. I can't help laughing at the look of fear on her face when she thinks about the prospect.

"You seriously think it's going to be harder than meeting me?" I quiz her.

"Yeah, I knew you'd be lovely, Jackson talks about you all the time" she states and I smile. "But those guys, that's a different kettle of fish altogether." She sighs.

"You'll be fine, they're lovely people," I offer. "What scares you? The fact they're an MC?" I ask. Sue's nod is almost imperceptible in reply. "It's nothing like you're imagining," I reassure her. "It's more like an old people's home than an MC." I chuckle, earning a reprimand from Jackson. It was worth it, and it's certainly broken the ice with Sue who looks a lot more comfortable now. "Didn't you meet them at my party?"

"No, I got there just before your mother arrived," she looks a little apologetic and unsure about whether she should have used the word mother.

"It's okay, carry on," I reassure her.

"Well, that kind of changed the mood so I stuck pretty close to Jackson after that. There were a few nods of hello and smiles but everyone just let us be."

"That's what they're like," I tell her. "Until they know you and they class you as part of the family, then they're always up in your face about your business, but in a good way," I smile. "Once they know you, they'll have your back." I promise her.

We chat movies, books and music and find that Sue and I have a lot of things in common. It's so nice to be able to talk about my favorite authors with someone who understands. Jackson normally looks at me like I'm speaking a foreign language when I talk about these things with him.

"I cried so hard at the end of 'A Star is Born'," she confesses and I agree with her.

"It broke me, what a sad ending." We both exclaim over Lady Gaga's voice and Jackson just sits there shaking his head. Apparently he'd gone with Sue and 'suffered through it' as he tells it. Sue gives me a conspiratorial wink and tells me he loved it really, although he'd never admit to it. My gentle giant has a soft side so I know she's right.

The evening ends far too quickly as they're heading off to see a movie. They invite me to join them but I politely decline. I'm shattered after my weekend adventures and am looking forward to a long soak in a hot bath, although I promise that I'll join them on another occasion.

Heading back to my car, I think about how much I enjoyed the meet up. I'm going to have to introduce Chris to them both at some point and cringe at the prospect. I just hope Jackson likes him as much as I like Sue!

CHAPTER TWENTY-FIVE

Rebel

I don't believe it. I stare at the flat tire on my car in disbelief. It was fine earlier. I could do without this. I pull my phone from my bag and am about to call Jackson when I remember he's on his way to the movies. I know he'd come sort this for me, but I don't want to spoil his evening. Instead I call the clubhouse. Finger's answers the phone. I let him know what's happened and he promises to send James and Harry out to fix it for me. I know I should just get on and sort it myself, but I'm in my work gear and don't fancy spoiling the manicure I paid so much for last week.

I head back to the office to wait for the lads, and remember I've run out of coffee pods. Damn, the bistro is still open so I could pop back in and get a takeaway coffee I guess. I

AVA MANELLO

leave it a moment, careful to give Jackson and Sue plenty of time to have left for the movies before I head in.

The waitress behind the counter grins at me. "You again?" She laughs. "Can't keep away from us today."

I explain about my car tire and she looks sympathetic, refusing to charge me for my coffee under the circumstances. I thank her and head back to the office.

It's not long before there's a knock on the door and Harry's face appears on the other side of the glass door. He's wearing another one of those horrid tracksuits of his. This one is a pale grey with white stripes and I just know he's going to get it filthy. I shake my head at his fashion sense. James on the other hand looks a lot more like a biker in his dark jeans, white tee and leather jacket. James greets me warmly whilst Harry appears slightly sullen in comparison. I chuckle to myself when I remember Jackson's nickname for him 'Triple B'. Jackson started calling him that a while ago and when I asked him what it meant he grinned from ear to ear when he explained "he think's he's Billy Big Bollocks so I call him triple B. Daft bugger thinks its some sort of compliment."

Harry definitely thinks he's better than he is, and he stands there shouting instructions at James as he gets out the spare tire and swaps it over for me. James needs no instruction, he's a mechanical whizz, spending most of his time in the workshop, tuning up the bikes. Harry on the other hand, I'm not sure I'd trust him to put out a fire in a swimming pool. I watch James as he silently works.

"I think someone cut your tire," he says quietly.

"Don't be daft." I reply. This town isn't like that. There's barely any petty vandalism.

"I'm serious." He shows me what could be a slit in the rubber. "I'll take it back and fix it for you, get it back in the morning just in case they decide to have another go." James is shy and often appears nice but dim in Harry's shadow, but I think that's more his innocence showing through. Because he's so quietly spoken, and rarely appears without Harry, he's often ignored and I think he may be vastly underrated.

"Thanks James," I offer him my hand. "I really appreciate this."

"Hey, what about me?" Harry blusters from his place against the wall, the same spot he's remained in watching James do all the hard work.

"Well, James is the one who swapped my tire over for me and is fixing the broken one. You've just lounged against that wall like a spare part," I reply. He starts to bluster and look offended but I just tune him out. I have no time for the Harry's of this world.

James waits until I'm safely in my car and on my way home before he gets back on his bike to return to the club-house. Harry is long gone. I watch the rear light of James's bike until it disappears before I turn my attention back to the main road. He can't have been right, I can't think why anyone would want to cut my tire. I must have driven over some broken glass or something.

Opening the front door I lean down to pick up the post and groan when I see a familiar envelope. This one has no postmark on it so must have been hand delivered. Eugh. When will they get the message. I toss it on the counter, along with the other post, there's nothing interesting in there, just bills and flyers.

I head for my en-suite and start running my bath. I spill a little too much bubble bath under the fast streaming tap and soon the bath is full of bubbles that threaten to over-flow the sides. Oops. Grabbing my Kindle and a glass of wine, I ease myself into the hot water, and let out a sigh of relief as the heat starts to ease the tension from my neck and shoulders. I open the book I'm reading and immerse myself in the psychological thriller. I've almost finished it and the plot line has caught me out a couple of times. This is my favorite kind of book. I think I've worked out a part of the plot, but the author has me second guessing myself every time I turn the page. Damn, I didn't see that coming.

The book is so addictive I have to finish it, only then do I realize how much the water has cooled. Ah well, I'll have wrinkly toes now. My glass of wine is barely touched, I'd become so deeply immersed in the plot I'd forgotten it was there.

I've been in the bath so long it's dark outside. I decide to forego watching any TV, instead opting for an early night. I head round the house, checking doors and windows are locked when again I notice something from the kitchen window. I'll have to investigate in the morning, as there's something out there again. I'm sure it's something innocent like the shadow of some garden furniture, but for a moment there it spooked me out.

Safely ensconced in my comfortable bed, I quickly forget whatever it was that I saw. I enjoyed the book I just finished so much I go online and buy the next in the series, it's a weakness of mine. I've only just started to get into it when my phone beeps with a message.

Jackson: Hey, James told me what happened. You okay?
Rebel: Yeah. I'm fine, he was brilliant, came straight out and fixed it.
Jackson: He say's someone slashed your tire.
Rebel: I'm sure I just drove over some glass or something without realizing it, I'm fine.
Jackson: Well, do your old man a favor and keep your eyes open just in case there's some nutter out there.
Rebel: Will do. By the way, I love Sue!
Jackson: Me too! Sleep well darlin' x

I HUG myself when I read Jackson's last line. He's not a man of many words, so to tell me he loves her too means this is something special. That's great to hear. I tut off the comment about a possible nutter out there. That kind of thing doesn't happen here, he's been watching too many movies. I'll just be a little more alert on my drive to work in the morning to make sure I miss whatever it was in the road that caused the flat.

Now, I have a book to read. As long as I don't fall asleep, I'm pretty sure I'll finish this in one sitting this time.

CHAPTER TWENTY-SIX

Rebel

The book I finished last night was good, too good, and I kind of regret finishing it now. It was two am before I got to sleep. Don't get me wrong, the book was more than worth it, but this hungover feeling from lack of sleep is going to stay with me all day. I should know better than to do this on a work night.

My first meeting isn't until ten am which means I can play hooky first thing, besides I still need to call at the store and stock up on coffee pods on my way in.

The shower does little to wake me, but the first hit of caffeine helps. Retrieving the bread from the toaster and opening the drawer for the butter knife I spot yesterday's post. I might as well tackle it now before I head into work. I'm sure I remember seeing the familiar logo of the card company in there. I can pay my statement whilst I eat breakfast.

Having sorted the bills and paid them, and discarded the flyers and junk mail only one envelope remains. Is there even any point in opening it and reading the same old, same old? As it was hand delivered I wonder if it was sent before or after they received my email. It wouldn't make sense to have sent it before, so I decide to open it and see what they have to say. Why they couldn't have just clicked reply on the email is beyond me.

The letter looks incredibly similar to the previous one, with one exception. They've raised the amount to $600,000 this time. I sigh in exasperation and open the email app on my tablet. I type out a firm but polite rejection of their offer, and advise them that they are wasting their time. There is no price that I am willing to sell at. I am not selling the land. I underline the last sentence to emphasize how serious I am about this. I follow this with a polite request for them to stop bothering me and sign off.

I wonder if Jackson had this much hassle with them, or did they just decide to approach me because I'm a potentially easier target. It doesn't matter really. I put the letter through the shredder in my office and as far as I'm concerned the matter is done with.

The letter has taken too much time and I haven't had chance to go check out the garden properly to see what keeps catching my eye on an evening when I lock up. I can't see anything obvious in the daylight. I'll have to wait and check when I get home this evening instead, although it might be a late one as I've agreed to meet my mom for dinner. I'm looking forward to seeing her again.

Chris is away on business so I haven't heard from him, but we have a date set for tomorrow night. I seem to have gone from doing nothing on a week night to being a social butterfly, having to check my diary to ensure I'm not double booking myself with all these engagements, but I wouldn't have it any other way.

THE STORE IS quiet when I head in and go straight to the coffee aisle. Damn, they're out of my favorite americano, but I settle for a grande instead. I only take the one box as I'm hoping Earl will order in my regular brand for me when I get to the counter. It should get me through today at least. I scan my eyes over the different offers and try and recall what Mrs. Jennings from the hotel prefers. Spotting the box of Chai Latte Tea I take one of those as well. I seem to remember she has a fondness for ginger biscuits so move to the next aisle to grab some of those for her.

Earl greets me warmly and promises me he'll have my coffee in for the morning for me. He's going to the wholesalers this afternoon. He even offers to drop it off at my office for me bless him, but I thank him and decline. I'm happy to call in on my way to work in the morning. He's ringing up my purchase when I hear the bell on the front door, turning my head in curiosity. It's a customer leaving without purchasing anything, I'm sure that looks like the back of George's head. It can't be, he doesn't work here in Maldon, or at least I don't think he does. I'm sure he said he was just here for a meeting. I turn back to Earl and apologize, asking him to repeat the question I just missed. He's asking about Jackson.

"He's well thanks, and I met his lady friend last night." I wink at Earl.

Earl's eyes open a little wider, Sue is obviously news to him. That shows how carefully Jackson has kept her under wraps as Earl knows all the gossip that goes on in town. We spend a few moments chatting about Sue, and Earl tells me he knows her, he's met her through the store owners association and he has only nice things to say about her. I'm glad she seems to be a popular member of the community.

MY MEETING with Mrs. Jennings took twice as long as needed, the business element was done with in the first ten minutes, but she loves to chat with me about her family and grandchildren as much as I love to hear about them. I think that's why my business does so well. I offer the same service a hundred other companies could provide, but I take the time to get to know my clients and to make them feel special. It's the little things that count, remembering the children's names and asking how they're doing, or just discussing their favorite TV show. I deliberately book more time out in the diary for these meetings than the work requires.

I spend the afternoon working on the proposals for Mrs. Jennings loan application, she wants to extend her guest house and the figures support it as I thought they would. I'll check with her which option she wants to go for, then submit the papers to the bank on her behalf. It's nice to know that I've contributed in some small way to the success of the town.

It's early evening when I leave the office ready to go meet my mom. I've freshened up in the bathroom and changed into a clean blouse, having spilled coffee on my other one. A car had backfired outside the office and I reacted badly, jumping in my seat. A moment earlier and I'd have been fine, the coffee had been on my desk, but as it was I'd just picked up the cup and was about to take a sip when it happened. This is why I keep a spare blouse in the office. I can be a bit of a klutz at times.

I don't believe my eyes when I step outside and see that I have another flat. This can't be happening. I'm sure I didn't drive over any glass or anything on my way in today, I'd been extra vigilant.

I drop a quick text to my mom to let her know I'm running late and why, then pick up the phone to the clubhouse again. It's James that answers this time and before I can say anything he apologizes for not bringing my spare tire back earlier. Damn, that's right, I don't even have a spare in the car to swap it over now, he took it away to repair it.

James agrees to come straight over and fix the tire for me, but his last words before he hangs up send a shiver through me.

"I'm sorry, Rebel, it was a slashed tire. Looks like someone doesn't like you."

CHAPTER TWENTY-SEVEN

Rebel

Thankfully James turned up on his own this time to repair the car. I'm not in the mood for Harry's snide comments and lazy attitude. It doesn't take him long to change the wheel over for me, and once again he offers to take the damaged wheel back with him to repair.

"It looks like it's been slashed again," he informs me, his voice full of regret and concern. He looks back at the front of my office and asks if I have any camera surveillance.

"It's not something I ever thought I needed," I reply. "I thought this was a safe location."

James nods his head in reply but suggests I report the two incidents to the police just in case. I promise to make a report in the morning. "Don't tell Jackson." I know I shouldn't ask him to keep this quiet, but I also know how over protective Jackson can be over things like this.

James looks at me with regret written all over his face. "You know I can't do that." Damn, James is too loyal. I'm pretty sure if it had been Harry here I could have bribed him to keep his mouth shut.

"It's okay, I shouldn't have asked you." I hug him to thank him for coming to my rescue again and feel his body freeze within my arms. The poor lad is so shy, I suspect he's still a virgin and definitely not used to female contact bless him.

I look my car over with suspicious eyes before I get in, other than the newly replaced wheel nothing seems out of sorts. I shake my head, there's no conspiracy here, just bad luck.

Mom looks pleased to see me when I finally make it to the restaurant and greets me warmly. It's still a little odd having her in my life, but she seems to have slotted into it so quickly considering just a short time ago I never knew she existed and then when I did, I didn't want to see her.

She grills me for information on my date with Chris and I happily share the PG version with her. She's not daft and can read between the lines of what I'm not saying though. I try and ask her about what it was like for her when she was dating and she shuts down a little.

"I wasn't allowed to date," she confesses. "I was called into the study one day and my father told me I was to be married. I don't think I saw Robert more than a handful of times before the wedding, and never just the two of us."

I can't think of anything worse. Not only did she have no say in the matter, there was no chance for her to find out if they were compatible.

"Weren't your feelings considered?" I ask as I toy with the pasta on my plate. I'm starting to lose my appetite, consumed with the unfairness of the situation she found herself in.

"My feelings weren't important, then or now." She sighs and puts her own fork down. "You have to understand, it was a different time, my father moved in important circles. It's what was expected. I guess you could say it's what I was born into."

"It all sounds so bloody Victorian," I protest. "Has he made you happy?"

"I've been comfortably provided for." Her reply evades the question. From the dull tone of voice she used I guess I already have the answer. I'm angry at her father, and Robert as well I guess, for what they've done to her. More importantly, what they've taken from her. Thinking about what's happening between me and Chris, she's missed out on all of that. The jittery nerves just before your date arrives, the anticipation, and then the mind blowing elation when you connect. Everyone should get to experience that in their life, even if it is only the once.

Mom sees the expression on my face and reaches over to

pat my hand. "Life isn't like a fairy tale, Rebel. We can't all live happily ever after. We can't all find a Prince Charming." I'm about to protest but she cuts me off. "It's okay. It is what it is."

I don't notice the tiny tear that has escaped my eye and is traveling down my cheek until she brushes it away for me. That small act of kindness makes my heart ache even more for her.

"Why don't you leave him?" I'm genuinely curious. There's a part of my mom where I can see how strong she is inside. I can't understand this docile accepting side of her. That's not who she is, or certainly not how she appears to me.

"Because I can't. I accepted this life, and now I have to live it."

"But…"

Again she cuts me off. "You need to understand that Robert is a powerful man. When he wants something he takes it, regardless of the cost. Robert wanted me and he got me, there's no way he will ever let me leave him." The way she says that is chilling. It makes him sound like some kind of monster. She reaches for the wine bottle and tops up her glass. Noticing my soda glass is almost empty she calls over the waitress to refill it. That's her unspoken way of telling me the subject is closed.

The rest of the meal is uncomfortable for me, not because I don't want to be here, but because I have to constantly bite my tongue, holding back the questions I'm desperate to ask and not uttering the offers of assistance. I want to help her escape this dreadful life she's living but she's shut down any attempt I've made to re-open the conversation. Jackson will know what to do, he always knows what to do. I'm sure he'll be able to help her. I hope he will anyway. This is a bit harder than a little girl running to her daddy with a boo boo on her knee. He can't just fix it with a kiss and a plaster, although I wish he could.

All I can do for now, until I've spoken to Jackson, is be her daughter. Let her be a part of my life, in whatever way she feels comfortable with.

I'm so busy overthinking everything that I miss the message tone on my phone. Mom notices though and glances at the screen. Her expression changes to one of concern and she slides the phone closer to my line of sight.

I gasp when I read the text.

Jackson: James got knocked off his bike on the way back to the clubhouse. He's in the hospital. Call me x

I dial Jackson's number with shaky fingers, listening to the ring tone that feels like it goes on forever. I let out the breath I've been holding when he finally answers.

"Hey darlin', they think he's going to be okay, he's still pretty dazed, but for some reason he keeps asking for you."

I look at my mom and before I can ask the question she's

gathering her things together and asking for the bill, ready for us to leave. "I'm on my way. What ward?"

"He's still in the emergency department, I'll text you if they move him to a room," Jackson advises.

"I've no idea why he wants me," I respond, "but I'll be there as soon as I can." I hang up on Jackson, give my Mom a quick hug and promise her I'll let her know what's happening before rushing out to my car.

The drive to the hospital seems to take forever, and I'm grateful to find a parking space in the crowded lot. The reception area is noisy and crowded and I can't see Jackson amongst the crowd. I'm just about to go over to the reception desk and enquire when I feel his arm on mine. He gives me a comforting hug before leading me back to the cubicle where James is.

I barely recognize him when I get there. He's covered in bruises and his face is swollen and scratched. His breathing is labored and he's wearing an oxygen mask to help him breathe. I look at Jackson in shock.

"It's not as bad as it looks darlin', he wasn't going fast as he was approaching a junction. Some guy ran a light and clipped the bike, knocking him off. They think he's broken his arm and got a concussion, but he's going to be okay." I move to the side of the bed and want to reach over and comfort James, but I'm scared of hurting him. His eyes open for a moment and he tries to smile when he sees me, but it obviously hurts too much.

"It's okay, I'm here now," I reassure him.

A nurse enters the cubicle and starts fussing over James, they're getting ready to move him to a ward so they can observe him overnight.

"Rebel," James struggles to talk, trying to move the oxygen mask aside so I can hear him. "Got to keep you safe Rebel." Before he can say anymore he's passed out again. What on earth does he mean he has to keep me safe? Safe from what?

CHAPTER TWENTY-EIGHT

Deidre

I feel sick with worry for Rebel. I'm sure the accident with James was no accident. I know Robert won't directly harm Rebel, or she wouldn't be able to sign over the land, but he'll think nothing of hurting those around her to get her to sign. Once she's signed... that doesn't bare thinking about.

As much as I love the time I spend with Rebel, and how we're getting closer, for some reason I feel lonelier than ever afterward. It doesn't make sense. I wonder if perhaps it's because I know that I cannot let this relationship flourish, as much as I want to, it's only going to bring harm to her.

My whole life I've been an afterthought, I don't remember being loved and cherished, or being anyone's first thought when they woke up. Everyone always had other priorities and I seemed to sit there, forgotten in the background. I'm a realist, I'm too old for that to happen now, and as I told Rebel, there's no such thing as Prince Charming. I just need to accept that this is what my life is and make the best of it, even if that means cutting Rebel out of it and breaking my heart in the process.

If Robert suspects I care anything for Rebel he will use that against me, another way to hurt me and inflict pain. He's an evil man. I've lost hours of sleep trying to think of a way to escape him, but it's just not possible. He has eyes in too many places, I'd never get away with it. Sometimes, when it's especially bad I pray that I won't wake from my sleep. Surely the nothingness that comes with death must be better than the sham of an existence I am forced to live each day.

Since I met Rebel I can't think like that anymore. I know I can't stay a part of her life, it's why I take as much pleasure as I can from these snatched moments we're allowed to share. I will have to live the rest of my life on memories. I did it before, I can do it again. I still cherish the memory of those dark brown eyes looking back at me as I held her as a baby, touching her skin so tenderly, afraid she'd break. She was a fragile and precious thing that I loved the instant that I saw her, my heart was hers from that first moment.

But that isn't my life. It may be for others, but it's one that wasn't meant for me. I'm not sure why, but I've been destined to walk a different path, a loveless path. I learned to be tough, to put on a good act, to cover the fact my heart was broken. I put on such a good act I started to believe it myself. And then I held my baby girl in my arms again, a grown woman this time, and greedily I want more. I want that life for me. I want to snatch more memories to keep me warm on those cold and lonely nights ahead. The nights where I lay there beaten and bruised, and everything hurts so much. No matter how hard the beatings though, nothing ever hurts as much as my heart.

I need to rebuild the walls I put around myself, to keep me safe. To embrace the numbness that got me through these years of abuse. It took so little for that wall to tumble when I saw her, so why is it so hard to re-build it now. I don't want to, but I know I have to. But please, God, just a little longer before I have to say goodbye, that's all that I ask.

I MUST HAVE DOZED off because I'm woken by a door slamming below and the sound of Robert shouting. He's drunk, I can hear the slur in his words. I can't make out who's on the receiving end of the tirade nor what it's about. Gingerly, I crack open my bedroom door. Light spills in from the hallway causing my eyes to wince at the unwelcome intrusion. It can't be Chris, as Robert has sent him off to deal with a problem with one of his network. Someone hasn't been paying up and he's sent Chris into making an example of him. No-one is allowed to make Robert look bad, there are always consequences regardless of how trivial the incident. My body bears testament to that, a network of scars catalogue the years of consequences I've paid for.

I can't hear what's going on properly, normally I'd ignore it and go back to bed, but this could be about Rebel. I edge cautiously along the landing, keeping in the shadows and careful not to make any noise. I can't get in a position to see, but I can hear them now and a shiver runs through me.

George is being yelled at because the young biker lived. What on earth? How far is Robert prepared to go to get Rebel to sign? I'd expected minor intimidation tactics, but killing people? She had the land signed over to her the other day, she's barely had time to get used to the idea. This is Robert all over, when he wants something he wants it yesterday, he has no patience. The spoiled brat of his childhood grew up to be a terrifying and evil man.

George is trying to argue his case, but there's no winning against Robert. The foolish boy should have learned that by now, but he's a fairly new recruit to Robert's stable of lackeys. It's no good, I need to get closer, the thick carpet does a good job of hiding my steps but it's not enough to silence the creak of the floorboard near the top of the stairs.

"Who's there?" Robert growls out.

"It's just me darling," I answer respectfully. "I was just going down to the kitchen to get a glass of milk." I move into his line of sight and wish I hadn't. The anger on his face is evident, the veins popping on his forehead. He looks like the monster that he is.

"Why are you sneaking around spying on me?" His words are cold and full of malice. I try not to cringe, he'll pounce on any sign of weakness. He feeds off it.

"I wasn't. I just wanted a glass of milk." I keep my voice pleasant and polite. Inside I'm a bag of nerves. "I didn't realize you had company, I'll leave you to it." I turn, trying to retreat and escape to my room, but it's too late. His anger has turned from George to me.

"Get down here, now," he hisses at me. "George, get the fuck out of here and don't come back till you've got results." A very relieved George rushes for the door, he doesn't even look back and offer me a look of sympathy.

I try and steel myself as I walk down the stairs as slowly as I can. I've heard that some victims can put themselves in a dissociative place during their abuse, they can go to some happy place in their head as their way of not being there in the moment. How I envy them. I've tried, believe me. I try and picture Rebel as a baby, those beautiful brown eyes looking at me, the soft feel of her skin. It only lasts a moment, the moment it takes for his fist to connect with my stomach leaving me doubled over in pain. Instead I curl my body in on itself, trying to minimize the area he can damage. There is no Prince Charming, this is my life.

CHAPTER TWENTY-NINE

Rebel

James has been out of it all night. They'd had to put him to sleep to set his arm as it's a complicated fracture. He looks so fragile laid in the hospital bed, his skin so pale against the stark white sheets, a drip in his arm feeding him pain relief. He's scratched and he's bruised, but aside from his arm he's going to be fine. I feel guilty, if he hadn't come out to rescue me this wouldn't have happened.

Jackson tried to persuade me to go home last night, but my guilt wouldn't let me. I know the guys from the club would have taken turns watching over him, but I refused. They've still come, but they're leaving me be, just coming into the room to let me know they're here and taking a silent watch in the hallway outside in case either of us needs anything.

Last I heard, the police hadn't found the truck that ran the light and hit him. I suppose the driver had been drinking, although it wasn't really late enough for that.

Dawn light is trickling through the curtains when Jackson comes back in, his face stern. "Okay, time for you to go home and get some sleep." He insists. When he uses that stern voice there's no arguing with him.

"Can't I at least stay until he wakes up?" I plead, knowing in advance how futile it is.

Jackson shakes his head in response. "You okay to drive or do you want me to take you?" He offers.

"Nah, I'll be fine. I've been dozing on and off in the chair." I stand and can feel the crick in my neck from the awkward sleeping position. I roll my shoulders to try and release it, but know that only a hot bath or shower will really help. I'll go home, freshen up, have a nap and come back.

Jackson escorts me to my car, I can't help noticing that he looks tired, I doubt he got much sleep himself last night. He gives me a hug, followed by a kiss on the forehead before I get in the car.

"Promise me you'll drive safe?"

I nod my head in reply.

As I pull out of the parking lot I see him walk back into the hospital, his shoulders slumped. That's not like him. He's normally so upbeat. I know he cares about everyone in the club, they're a huge extended family, but I think he has a soft spot for James. I don't know James's history, he's never shared with me, but I think he did with Jackson. Whatever it is, I get the impression it wasn't good. I know if the club hadn't taken him in he had nowhere else to go. That saddens me, but I do know he has family now that care for him and will look after him. They'll take the piss out of him of course, and write obscenities and insults on his cast, but that's just how they are. At the end of the day, they'll always have his back.

I hadn't realized how tired I was and I'm so grateful when I finally pull onto my driveway. I'm not sure whether to just go straight to bed or shower then bed. The comfort of my mattress wins out and I don't even bother removing my clothes, just my shoes.

FROM THE AMOUNT of sun filling my room I've slept for a while, a glance at the clock confirms it. It's almost eleven am. As much as I want a shower, the need for coffee is more important right now. I pad barefoot into the kitchen and switch on the coffee machine. I choose a grande from the pots in the carousel beside the machine. I need a bigger cup this morning. There's something about the smell of fresh coffee, I inhale the aroma and immediately feel better. I'm about to take my coffee to the shower with me when I notice some post on the doormat. That wasn't there this morning when I came in and the postman doesn't come until mid afternoon. It must have been hand delivered. I groan at the familiar envelope. When will they realize I am not selling. I toss the offending envelope on the kitchen table and head for my en-suite.

The knot in my neck eases slightly under the hot steaming flow of water, but doesn't go away completely. It's more than just sleeping awkwardly in a chair, I'm pretty sure it's stress as well. The slashed tires, James's accident and this constant hassle from the developers are getting to me.

I dress for the office, determined to make a detour to the hospital on my way in, but notice that Jackson has sent me a text. James has woken up and they're releasing him. As they'll be just sat around waiting for release paperwork and could be a while Jackson suggests I go visit at the clubhouse this evening instead. I text a reply confirming I'll pop by after work.

Earl greets me warmly when I pop in to the store to collect my order of Americano. He's heard about the accident and asks after James.

"Weird as anything, we only ever seem to have accidents like that when the place is full of tourists," he muses. He's right. Outside of the main tourist season it's normally pretty peaceful here, even in tourist season it's not that bad. The odd pickpocket attracted by the crowds or a drunken brawl after a day full of boozing.

"There's always a first time," I offer.

Something seems off about my office as I pull into the street, I can't quite make it out. It's only as I get closer that I see the huge plank of wood over the window. What the hell? I park up in my usual spot and jump out. Mr. Andrews from the gift shop next door rushes out to greet me.

"Rebel, I'm so glad I caught you." He looks worried. "I'm afraid your window was smashed this morning when I got here. I called the glazier and he came and put some wood up for you, I swept up what I could from outside, but I think you're going to find most of it inside."

I don't understand what's going on here. All these accidents. I look down the rest of the street and realize mine is the only window damaged. Mr. Andrews sees me looking. "Yeah, it's odd that, yours was the only window damaged. I couldn't get inside so couldn't work out what caused it. Figured we'd take a look when you got here and we could see if you needed to call the police. Might be something as innocent as a bird." I can tell he doesn't believe it was a stray bird that caused the damage. "I heard about the accident last night so figured you'd be a little late in, I was going to call you at lunchtime to see what you wanted to do about it."

Bless him, I appreciate what he's done for me. Together we head into the office and I have to switch the light on as the wood on the window has made it so dark in here. There's broken glass all over the floor behind the window so something came through it that's for sure. I look around to see what it was whilst Mr. Andrews heads back to his store for a brush, dustpan and gloves. He's left strict instructions that I am not to pick up any of the shards of glass with my bare hands.

The rock is in the corner, it's heavy enough to have done the damage, but not something that would just have been lying around on a street outside. Someone would have had to bring this with them, this wasn't just spur of the moment opportunistic vandalism, this was pre-meditated. Why was mine the only window smashed?

Mr. Andrews spots the rock in my hand when he comes back in. "I'm calling the police."

CHAPTER THIRTY

Rebel

W ell, that was a waste of time. The policeman wasn't really interested, he gave me a reference number for the insurance company but doesn't seem to think they'll catch the offender. Out of curiosity I mentioned that I'd had my tires slashed two days in a row, but he still thinks it's some petty kids having a laugh at my expense. Even if they do find them, chances are they'll get nothing more than a caution.

The glazier will be back tomorrow as he had to order the glass in. It's too dark and gloomy in the office with the boarded up frontage, so there's not much chance of getting much work done. Mr. Andrews, bless him, insisted on cleaning up the glass for me before he would go back to his own store. He also said he would raise the problems I've been having at the next store keepers meeting as there's one in a few days. You never know, someone might have seen something, although I'm not holding my breath.

Dealing with the broken window took longer than I thought it would, but at least it means it's probably a good time to head over to the clubhouse and see how James is doing. I'm relieved when I lock the office door to see that the tires on my Kia are intact today. That makes a nice change. What has my life come to when I'm grateful my tires are intact. I shake my head in dismay.

The clubhouse is busy when I enter, looks like everyone had the same idea of cutting work early to welcome James home. I find him in a corner being fussed over by a few of the old ladies. I have to chuckle, the poor lad isn't used to this much attention.

"I'll be fine, honest," he protests, trying to brush them away with his good arm. His face lights up in relief when he spots me. "Rebel, thank god you're here, tell them I'll be fine. It's only a few scratches!"

If I wasn't feeling so guilty for him having his arm in a cast, I'd have been tempted to toy with him and encourage the over solicitous behavior, instead I assure Daisy, Cilla and Smokey that he'll be fine. I'll keep an eye on him for a bit. There's a little lighthearted muttering, and after promising them they can make us a sandwich and a drink we finally get rid of them.

"So how are you?" I ask, looking over at the various bruises that have darkened since last night and the multitude of scratches James is sporting.

"Relieved if that makes sense," he offers. I tilt my head in question as I'm not sure what he means. How can you be relieved at having been knocked off your bike? He sees my confusion and helps me out. "I'm relieved because it could have been a hell of a lot worse. The truck wasn't going fast enough to cause serious damage. Like me my bike's a little battered and bruised but nothing that won't fix. I was lucky," he finishes quietly.

Now I understand. A truck versus a bike doesn't normally end well, and it's rarely the bikers fault. You have to have a sixth sense out on the road, not only do you have to be on constant alert, you've got to assume the other guy is going to pull out of that junction or cut you off. James tells me he'd caught the truck in the corner of his eye and tried to brake, but hadn't been quick enough to avoid it.

"It's odd, I'm sure I saw it parked up when I arrived to fix your tire. Guess it was just bad luck and timing that he chose to set off at the same time as me." He shrugs.

"Well, it wasn't a slashed tire today," I tell him, "when I got to work today my office window had been smashed in."

"Who the hell is doing this to you? You've got to call the police." He sounds concerned and I'm quick to reassure him that that's exactly what I did.

"Old Mr. Andrews next door called them. They think it's kids, and that they'll soon get bored of picking on me." I hope so, it's not the money as much as the inconvenience they're causing that upsets me. Not to mention that thanks to their stupid little prank James is now sporting a cast, but as he says, it could have been so much worse.

"I'm not so sure it is kids," James offers. "There's something about the way those tires were slashed. I don't think kids would have done that. They'd have been much messier. This was neat and precise. You need to watch your back, Rebel, especially now they've smashed your window. You need to tell Jackson."

"Tell Jackson what?" Jackson's hands come to rest on my shoulders and he reaches down to kiss me on the cheek before turning his attention back to James.

"Erm, I, erm.." Poor James always turns into a jabbering mess in front of Jackson, bless him.

"Nothing important," I save his stutters. "I've had a couple of tires slashed and my office window smashed." I can see Jackson is about to interrupt so rush out my last few words to make sure I get them in and he hears them, 'but the police have been called and they think it's just kids playing a prank."

"I don't think so," James finally finds his voice.

"Don't be silly," I respond. "This isn't Victoria, it's Maldon. It's a quiet little town with no trouble. I'm sure the officer was right and it's just kids pratting around. Hopefully they saw the police there earlier and will give it a rest." What is it with men overreacting to everything? The police weren't concerned and that's good enough for me, there's no need for me to be concerned either.

Jackson doesn't seem convinced though, and I spend the next hour trying to reassure him and talk him out of assigning a bloody security detail to me. I also refuse to come stay at the clubhouse just to allay his fears.

"Jackson, I'm thirty. I have my own home and business. I can take care of myself. I do not need a babysitter." I don't raise my voice to him, but I am firm. I refuse to be coddled like a child over this.

"But," before he can finish I've cut him off.

"No, and that is my final answer." He looks at my solemn face and nods, reluctantly. I know that no matter how annoying he is being right now, it's because he cares and he wants to keep me safe. "I'm the one that spoke to the police, and if they're not worried then neither should you be."

Jackson keeps eyeing me across the table as James and I play Scrabble on my iPad. James is one of the few people I enjoy playing with as he's a ringer. He may not look overly clever, but he has a sharp mind and an extensive vocabulary. Trying to beat him is always a challenge, but an enjoyable one. I really must learn more two letter words as he's the master of them and they're the key to the high scores he comes up with. I groan as he places his final tile, once again he's scored over 350 and I'm lucky to have 297. I need to spend less time watching Criminal Minds and more time reading the scrabble dictionary.

187

CHAPTER THIRTY-ONE

Rebel

C hris is back from his trip away, but he sounded so tired on the phone that we decided to just have a chilled out evening with a pizza and a movie. I know it's only been a few days since I saw him, but it feels like forever. Work dragged today so I cut out early once the glazier had finished and popped over to the clubhouse to check up on James. He's fine, just a little bored, so I left him with some crossword books to keep his brain occupied. I hadn't really thought it through though as it's his right arm that he writes with and that's the one he broke. Still, the thought was there I grin to myself.

I busy myself flitting from room to room, duster in my hand making sure my home looks the best it can. I'd already blitz cleaned yesterday when I got back from the clubhouse as I'd needed to keep busy, too busy to think about the messed up things that were happening around me.

When I finish and head back to the kitchen to put away the cleaning stuff I groan as I spot another bloody envelope on the door mat again. Why won't they get the message. I'm sick of emailing them and telling them no. I'm not even opening this one. I refuse to give them any more of my time. Snatching the offending item, I head straight for my desk and feed it into the shredder. No… this bloody envelope is as annoying now I'm treating it as trash as it was before. I may have a decent shredder but it's not equipped to take a fully stuffed envelope and it grinds to a halt with only a fraction of the envelope caught in the mechanism. Reaching for the plug, I disconnect the shredder and spend the next twenty minutes trying to disentangle the jammed envelope. By the time I am finished the floor is a mess of shredded paper that resembles grimy confetti, but at least the shredder is working again. I sweep the tiny pieces of litter from the floor and discard them in the kitchen bin when I catch sight of the time on the kitchen clock and shriek when I realize Chris will be here soon. I'm not ready. I'm a hot and sweaty mess. I run for the shower, hoping I can get ready in time.

I've managed to dress in jeans and a tee but not dry my hair when there's a knock at the door. Damn. Still, I guess this was supposed to be a chill night. I pad bare foot to the door and can't help the grin that lights up my face as I open it to Chris.

"Now there's a sight for sore eyes," he croons. He pulls me in for a kiss that I feel right down to my toes. I really missed him. It's only when he pulls his hand from behind his back that I notice he was hiding something. He hands me a gift bag and I accept it. The top has been taped shut and I take my time appreciating the packaging, trying to guess from the weight and shape what could be inside. "Just open it," he says, his voice full of laughter.

The parcel has some weight to it, but it doesn't feel heavy or solid. I grab the scissors from the drawer and snip the tape open. It looks like a cuddly toy. Curious I lift it from the bag and let out a yelp of delight when I see what he's bought me.

"He's called Rebel Lion," Chris tells me. I saw him and he made me think of you.

I'm laughing as I check him out. His long furry mane has been spiked up and he's wearing a heavy studded collar over his incredibly soft fur, but the best part is the small leather biker jacket he's wearing. He's a biker lion. The small cardboard tag on his ear has some facts on about baby lions. His gold mane has traces of black at the edges, and turns into a long black beard under his chin which follows down into a soft creamy belly. His long golden tail is floppy and is tipped with more dark brown. He's large enough to fill my arms, but small enough to cuddle. I skip over to the sofa and sit down, hugging my new toy to me. Chris huffs as he realizes I'm showing more attention to the soft toy than I am to him.

"I love him, he's perfect. But where on earth did you find a biker lion?" I ask, still examining him in close detail.

"I didn't, I had to go to three different stores for this," he explains. "I saw the lion in a gift store as I was passing, then sought out a pet store for his collar and found a trendy baby store for the leather jacket so he really is a one off, just like you." Chris finishes his sentence by moving in and kissing me, squishing the lion against my chest. "Now I think he's had enough of your attention for this evening," he chuckles, taking Rebel Lion from my arms and putting him in a chair across the room where he sits, slightly lopsided watching us as we say hello properly.

We're interrupted by a knock at the door, it's the pizza I ordered earlier. I carry the boxes back to the sofa and pass Chris his mighty meat feat whilst I inhale the aroma of my stuffed crust margarita and all its cheesy goodness. I grab the remote and switch to the movie channel, I've already rented the movie as I remember Chris saying he wanted to see it but had missed it at the cinema. His face lights up when he sees the titles roll across the screen. He's a massive Star Wars geek and I've rented the latest movie, Solo, for him. I'm looking forward to this one as it's the story before Star Wars and is all about how Hans and Chewie met. When I see Chewbacca appear on the screen he makes me think of my new gift. I love that Chris thought about me whilst he was away, and the trouble he went to in order to make that gift something unique to me.

"Oh!" I exclaim. "I've just twigged what his name is. Rebel Lion... put it together and you have Rebellion, you named him after me!" I'm taken aback at the extra thought over the name as well.

This man is a keeper. I've never felt that way about anyone before, but there's a connection there that I've never felt with anyone else. He's the other half of me.

"You were a bit slow on the uptake there." He's laughing with me, not at me. I shove him in the shoulder, but before I snuggle up close with him to watch the movie I cross the room and retrieve my gift.

I return to the sofa, leaning into Chris on one side with my feet up and Rebel Lion in my arms on the other. Chris looks at the half eaten pizza in front of me. "You not finishing that?" He's devoured all of his.

"Nah, it tastes even better in the morning for breakfast," I reply.

"You're not serious?" He sounds disgusted.

"You're telling me you've never eaten cold pizza for breakfast?" I sit up shocked. "Well, shut up and watch this movie I put on for you and in the morning I will introduce you to the delicacy that is leftover pizza." I grin at him.

"Oh, so I'm staying over now am I?" His voice is full of amusement.

"Of course," I give him my best seductive smile but suspect it comes off as more of a grimace judging by the way he falls about laughing.

"Cold pizza it is then." He pulls me back into him and we

snuggle up to watch the rest of the movie, my lion comfortably close on my other side. It's a good movie, but I'm definitely looking forward to the post movie entertainment more.

CHAPTER THIRTY-TWO

Rebel

By the time we surface from the bedroom it's more like brunch than breakfast. Chris is eying the cold pizza with uncertainty.

"It doesn't even have any meat on it," he complains.

"Shut up and try it," I chastise. He's like a petulant child this morning.

"Do I have to?" He whines and I dissolve into a fit of giggles. He picks up the slice of pizza hesitantly and takes the tiniest bite. I've seen toddlers eat more. He follows this with a larger bite and then tries the stuffed crust. "Hey, this isn't half bad." He's talking with his mouth full, but I'll forgive him on this one occasion.

"Told you so." I laugh at him.

Chris enjoys the cold pizza so much he eats it all before I've returned to the table with the freshly brewed coffee. "That was supposed to be for both of us!" I whine.

"Oops. Sorry, it was good though." He gives me the cheekiest grin and I can't stay angry at him for long, even if I wanted to. I get back up and head to the fridge, hoping I have some bacon in there. I'm rewarded with bacon, eggs and mushrooms. Chris accepts wholeheartedly when I offer him a cooked breakfast. I can't believe he has room for it after all that pizza, but then he was pretty active last night... in the bedroom, in the shower and then back in the bedroom. Okay, and this morning as well. I guess he burned off enough energy to warrant the extra nutrition. I'm grinning widely as I chop the mushrooms and add them to the butter in the frying pan. Chris comes up behind me and wraps me in his arms, nuzzling my neck. I hate that I have to shoo him away when it's time for me to concentrate on frying the eggs. I make him work by asking him to put the bread in the toaster. Happy that the eggs are cooking okay I pop the baked beans into the microwave, then turn the bacon. The kitchen smells amazing. There's nothing to beat a cooked breakfast after a night of indulgence.

I set the plates on the table and Chris thanks me. "This looks amazing." We don't talk whilst we eat, although we share a lot of smiles and grins. Plates empty I clear them away and Chris stands beside me at the sink, drying the pots and putting them away as I wash them.

"So when do I get to meet Jackson?" Chris's question is so

unexpected I drop the plate I'm holding and watch it bounce on the kitchen floor, thankfully it doesn't break so I put it back in the bowl and wash it again.

"You want to?" I ask doubtfully. "Isn't it a bit early days for that?"

"You and I both know that what we have isn't normal, Rebel. So yeah, I'd like to meet him."

I finish washing the pots in silence, contemplating what Chris has asked. I've never formally introduced anyone I was seeing to Jackson, granted he's met a few when they called at the clubhouse to collect me when I was younger, but no one since then. No one lasted long enough. I unconsciously twist my lips as I remember one boy from college that had a run in with Jackson. I guess Chris should know what he's asking for. Pots finished I direct Chris to the sofa and sit cross legged facing him, hugging my toy lion in my arms.

"What's wrong, Rebel?" Chris asks, his voice laced with concern.

"I think there's something you should know about Jackson before you meet him." I start. "Now, bear in mind that what I'm about to tell you I didn't know about at the time, I only found out a couple of years ago when I bumped into Brett."

"Who's Brett?" Chris interrupts. I'm sure that's jealousy I see on his face.

"He's no one," I reassure him. "Just someone I used to

know. Now shut up and listen, no interrupting," I chastise him. Chris gives me a suitably appropriate look and sits back, quietly. I think back to the conversation I had with Brett when I bumped into him, I'm still not sure whether to laugh at what he told me or be pissed as hell with Jackson, even after all these years. I shift on the sofa, getting comfortable so I can tell Chris what he's up against.

"Okay, this story goes back to when I was at college. I was seeing this guy called Brett, it wasn't anything serious, but we were exclusive. I came home one day in tears because I'd caught him kissing Sandra Levinski in the bleachers. She had a bit of a reputation for being easy, and I guess as I'd refused to sleep with him he'd looked elsewhere. I wouldn't have been so upset if he'd finished with me first, but we were still together. I was really upset, what with everything with my mother abandoning me I was quite sensitive when it came to relationships. I doubt Brett even thought about what he was doing, but to me he was telling me loud and clear that I wasn't good enough for him. I was pretty inconsolable. Anyway, Jackson found me and finally persuaded me to tell him what was wrong. He promised he wouldn't do anything, that he'd let me sort it out myself and I believed him. I didn't need anyone fighting my battles for me. I saw Brett at college the following morning and told him we were over. He kind of went out of his way to avoid me after that, but I never thought anything of it. I didn't realize for a long time that I never heard about him dating after that. As far as I was concerned he was nothing to me, and I didn't listen in when his name was brought up in conversations.

A couple of years ago I bumped into him at a conference, and for old times' sake we had a drink and a catch up. He was engaged and just about to get married to a lovely girl he'd met through his work and he even invited me to the wedding." Chris is looking at me in confusion, he doesn't know where this story is going or how it's relevant to Jackson. "Just bear with me, I'm almost there," I promise. "So Brett asked me if Jackson had ever told me what happened between them. I obviously didn't know what he was talking about so he went on to tell me. Jackson had collared him that next day after college and asked if he could help him with a job. He needed an extra pair of hands. Brett didn't see any harm in it and thought he might earn a few dollars so agreed. They called at the storage shed and picked up a shovel and pick and a tarpaulin sheet then they drove for miles, into the middle of nowhere. Jackson pulled the truck to a stop and said that this was the spot. He stood against the truck and watched whilst Brett dug a hole in the dry earth. After a an hour of digging Brett was exhausted and asked how much bigger he had to make the hole. Jackson just grinned at him and told him to make it big enough so he could fit in it, and deep enough that he'd never be found. As you can imagine that freaked Brett out. Jackson then explained that no one cheated on his daughter and got away with it. He told him to keep digging, the hole wasn't big enough. Brett lost it, he dropped to his knees and sobbed for forgiveness. Once Jackson was sure the message had got home he let Brett up, told him that if promised never to cheat on a woman again he'd let him fill up the hole and they could go home and forget this had ever happened, along with a proviso that I wasn't to find out. Of course Brett agreed. He genuinely believed that Jackson was going to put him in that hole and leave him there. Apparently it had such an impact on him that he stopped messing around, he even stopped dating for a while, he was that scared of Jackson. Anyway, he eventually met his fiancée and everything was fine. So…" I pause the story to look Chris in the face. "You sure you still want to meet Jackson?"

CHAPTER THIRTY-THREE

Rebel

C hris looks a little white when I finish my story. His Adam's apple visibly moves as he takes a breath before answering me.

"I've met some protective fathers in my time," he admits, "but that's a whole new extreme to me." He shakes his head a little. "Got to admire the guy though, and yes, he sounds like someone I'd love to meet." I let out the breath I've been holding. I didn't want to scare Chris off, but he already means something to me and I felt it was only fair to warn him what he was in for.

"You up for today? I want to call in and check on James anyway."

Chris looks at me curiously. "Who's James?" There's a coldness to his voice that I've not heard before.

"He's one of the guys at the clubhouse, he was knocked off his bike the other night when he came out to help me so I kind of feel responsible. I just want to go see how he's doing."

Chris seems to accept the explanation and relaxes a little, then I see a question flit across his face. "Why did you need help?"

"My tire was slashed and James came out to swap it over for me, it happened two nights in a row but the police seem to think it was just kids pranking me." I'd forgotten to tell Chris about the events of the last few days, I'd just been so glad to see him it had slipped my mind.

"Police? What's going on?" Now I hear concern.

"Nothing really, like I said, the police think it's just kids. They put my office window through as well." I shrug my shoulders, indicating that it isn't something I'm overly concerned about.

"Why didn't you tell me?"

"You were away with work, it wasn't anything serious. I didn't think it was important enough to bother you with."

Chris nods his head in understanding but he seems to be upset over what I perceive to be nothing more than a storm in a teacup. "I just worry about you is all." He places a soft kiss on my forehead.

"Right, best get ready to go meet Jackson and my other dads' then." I jump up from the sofa and head to the bedroom, ignoring Chris's groan at the thought of meeting not just one but a multitude of fathers in one go. Is it wrong that I get a thrill of pleasure at his obvious discomfort? It was his idea after all. I grab my Vans and some trainer socks along with my purse. I haven't got a gift for James today, hopefully the entertainment of watching Jackson size up Chris will be enough for him.

Chris reluctantly agrees to go in my car when I tell him it will be easier to get through the gates, they know my vehicle. He's a nervous passenger though, braking with his feet well before I do. I chuckle at him to begin with, but by the time we're close to the clubhouse it's getting slightly annoying.

"Will you stop braking for me!" I shout in frustration the next time he does it.

"But you brake so late," he protests.

"I brake in plenty of time, you sound like a bloody woman driver. Man up!" I chastise him. He gives me a look of apology and does try. The next time I brake he starts to move his foot unconsciously but stops himself just in time.

As we approach the clubhouse gates it's like Chris changes in front of me. He straightens up and his whole body stiffens. The closest thing I can think of is an actor getting into character before he goes on stage. "You're not at work, Chris. The best thing with these guys is to be yourself, the man you are when you're with me. They won't be impressed by you any other way," I suggest.

He takes a moment to consider what I've said, by the time I've driven through the gates he looks more like the Chris I know and love. I find it a little sad that he feels he needs two personas to get through life. Personally, I'm just me, take me or leave me.

I link my arm through Chris's as we enter the clubhouse, returning greetings. I'd expected a sudden silence and all heads to turn towards us, but it didn't happen for which I'm grateful, although knowing my dads' they're probably already aware of what Chris is to me and it wouldn't surprise me if they had a record of every time he's stayed over. I know they do these things because they care, but occasionally it gets a little stifling.

Daisy, Fingers' old lady comes over to hug me and eyes Chris up and down in appreciation, giving me a wink when she thinks he's not looking.

"Why was Fingers on the gate today?" I ask. It's normally James or Harry's job to man the gate.

"Harry seems to have gone walkabout," she tuts in disgust. She's a school teacher so has the disapproving tut off to a tee. "Went out for a ride last night and no one has heard from him since, lazy fekker." I chuckle. Daisy always sounds so refined, even when she swears and it always makes me laugh. "So, you going to introduce me to this fine young man or not young lady?"

I carry out the formal introductions and Daisy appraises Chris for a moment, before unexpectedly throwing her arms round him and hugging him. "Welcome to the family."

Chris looks a little surprised, as am I. I wasn't expecting that from Daisy. I guess her experience as a teacher helps her quickly weigh up people when she first meets them. She obviously approves of Chris. I look around to see if I can spot Jackson but he doesn't appear to be in the main area. Daisy catches my eye and lets me know I'll find him in his office. Telling Daisy I'll catch up with her later, I drag Chris along behind me until we're outside Jackson's door. Even I feel nervous now, I guess this is a big thing for me after all. I gulp in a deep breath to steady myself before knocking on the door. Jackson shouts out that it's okay to enter. Grasping a tighter hold of Chris's hand I stick my head around the corner of the door.

"Hey, you got a minute for me?" I greet him with my widest smile.

"Always for you darlin'."

I pull Chris in after me. "I've got someone I'd like you to meet." I introduce the two main men in my life to each other and hold my breath, watching them closely to see how they react to each other. Jackson looks a little wary at first, he must know how important this is to me. I just hope he doesn't start posturing and being full of bravado. Chris greets him respectfully, and with a firm but friendly handshake which Jackson returns.

I visibly relax as they're soon deep in conversation with

each other, practically ignoring me. I've no idea what they're talking about as it's something over my head, so decide to leave them to it and go visit with James. They almost miss me leaving the room until I raise my voice and tell them where I'm going. They don't even bother speaking to me, just nod their heads and go back to their chat.

Men! Remind me again why we put up with them?

CHAPTER THIRTY-FOUR

Rebel

J ames is almost back to himself today. He's a stronger man than most people give him credit for. There's still a little stiffness in the way that he carries himself, thanks to residual bruising and pain, but he's pottering around doing the jobs that he can. I admire him, it must be frustrating as hell to know you're not allowed out on your bike. I haven't been out on mine since before my party, life just seems to have taken over. I need to put that right, but at least I can. James is in good spirits although he's concerned that Harry didn't return last night.

"There's something wrong, Rebel, but they just keep telling me it's typical Harry." He brushes a hand through his curly mop of hair, frustration written all over his face. "I know he can be a bit of a lazy sod, and a shirker some-times, but this isn't that."

"I'm sure he'll come waltzing in before I leave with some fantastic story about whatever adventure he was up to last night." I try and reassure him. "Let's not forget, his wing man is out of action so he'll have been bored."

"Maybe." James seems to consider what I've said, but I can tell his heart isn't in his answer, he doesn't really believe that's the case.

"How are the crosswords coming along?" I'm stunned when he tells me he's finished both books already. He really must have been out of his mind with frustration since I dropped them off.

"They're not as challenging or as much fun as when I'm whupping your ass at Scrabble." He laughs at me. I'm about to punch him in the arm for that comment but pull back just in time as I'm sat on the same side as his broken arm.

"You want challenging?" I gesture to Jackson's office. "Try sitting here whilst your other half is being grilled by your dad." I roll my eyes and James roars with laughter.

"Now that's something I'd love to see." James cocks his head in my direction and looks at me. "Hang on a minute, when did you get an other half?"

I raise my eyes, unsure how to answer. I guess from the outside this has all been pretty quick, a few weeks ago I was as single as you can be and now I'm sitting here all loved up. I'm about to answer when we're disturbed by the entrance of Jackson and Chris.

If I didn't know better I'd swear they'd been pals for life, they're doing that man hug thing and bumping knuckles. Aside from the fact they look bloody ridiculous, I'm taken aback. This isn't quite what I expected when I left them together. Granted, I'm pleased that they like each other, but this whole best buddy vibe they're giving off is a touch unsettling. No good can come of it, I'm pretty sure it will translate into them tag teaming up against me and taking the piss out of me constantly.

Looking at the two favorite men in my life, I choose to accept my fate, if that's what it's going to be like then bring it on. I love these guys unconditionally and am so happy that they appear to be getting on.

Chris sits down beside me, so close I can feel the heat from his thigh against mine, then reaches around me, pushing me back into the seat so he can greet James. "Hi, you must be James. Nice to meet you. How are you feeling, Rebel told me about your accident. That sucks man."

I sit there dumbfounded as I watch James fall under his spell as well. Not only has Chris just slotted right into my life outside of the club, he appears to fit perfectly here as well. I don't believe in fate, but perhaps this was meant to be after all.

Jackson stays for a short while, mainly to make sure James is okay, before excusing himself as he has some business to attend to. Chris stands to say goodbye and they promise to meet up soon, just the two of them, for a drink. They're already planning nights out without me? Pfft.

I'm so wrapped up in my pissed off mood that I tune out of the conversation. They don't appear to need me, they're happy amongst themselves. Apparently Chris plays chess so James has finally found someone who understands him. I've tried, I really have, but there are so many rules and I've always thought it was such an old man game that I've never given it the time it needed to learn the game.

My attention is caught when they start talking about James's accident. As he describes the truck that hit him it triggers a spark of a memory. I'm sure I've seen that truck around recently, and it stood out for some reason. The more I try and grab hold of the memory the more elusive it becomes.

"I wish I could remember where I've seen it." I say almost absently.

"Yeah, Harry thought it sounded familiar as well. I'm sure that's where he was going last night, he had an idea where it might be and he wanted to go check it out and see if there was any damage on it." James's concern is infectious.

"Any idea where he'd seen it?" Chris asks, his tone suddenly switched from jovial to business.

"I think he said it was up near the old Sanders place." I can see that James is straining to remember more of his conversation with Harry, but nothing is coming to him either.

"Then we should go look for him," I state, standing

quickly and jostling James's broken arm in the process. "Oh, I'm so sorry," I apologize. James brushes it off as nothing.

"I don't think you should go." Chris looks at me, concern in his eyes. "It might not be safe for you."

He didn't just play the little woman card did he? I straighten my back and look him in the eye, fury in my voice. "Do not underestimate me. My friend is missing, and I'm going to look for him. He might be hurt. You're welcome to come with me," I offer, "but make no mistake, I'm going."

James sits there looking between us, his head turning from side to side as though he's watching a tennis match, silently laughing at the show in front of him. "Can I come too?" He asks.

"Yeah, you coming Chris?" I pick up my bag, pulling my car keys out and holding them in my hand as I walk towards the door. Chris huffs his shoulders in submission and follows behind me.

James gets into the car fine and just needs a little assistance with his seat belt, but we're soon on the way. Once again Chris insists on driving and I ignore him. He needs to learn that I am not some fragile wallflower, I grew up in an MC and was taught how to look after myself from an early age. As we head out of the gate I turn left, the opposite direction to my home. This stretch of road is quiet and doesn't see a lot of through traffic. The club and surrounding properties are set in a large remote rural area.

Unless you're visiting one of the properties there's no real cause to be out here.

We've not driven very far when Chris asks me to slow down. I'm not sure what he's seen but I apply the brakes regardless. "There's what looks to be some tire marks on the road." He indicates through the windscreen and I see what he means. I try and remember if there were there the last time I was out on this road, but can't. The markings look like thick black rubber treads from something braking too quickly. James has his face to the passenger window, scanning the roadside and Chris is looking towards the front. The road is sparsely lined with trees and there's a large drainage ditch either side behind the tree line.

"Stop here, I think I see something." Chris instructs me in a soft voice, all the bluster and command from earlier gone. A chill passes through me. "No, stay here, please?" He begs me as I go to get out of the car. There's something in his tone that glues me to my seat. I agree to stay put, for now.

James releases the seatbelt with his good arm and gets out of the car with Chris. I watch, dread in my heart as they walk a little ahead of the vehicle and move towards the ditch. That's when I see it. The twisted remains of a motor-bike are barely visible against the dry grass, seated deep within the ditch. How did I not see it before? I can't stay here knowing that Harry may be in that ditch and needing our help.

I really wish I hadn't left the car. When I reach the top of the ditch I can see the shreds of fabric, it looks like denim but the dark stains on it look black in the shady light beneath the tree. I follow the fabric upwards.

"Shall I call an ambulance?" I ask, my voice trembling with unshed tears. James is backing away from the sight in front of him, and bumps into me. Silent tears fall down his face. It's only when I feel the damp on my own cheeks that I know I'm crying as well.

"It's too late for that," Chris sighs. "Call the police, I don't think this was an accident."

CHAPTER THIRTY-FIVE

Chris

Rebel is a mess and I hate that she had to see that. I'd tried to persuade her to return to the car whilst we waited for the police to arrive, but she refused. She stood there hugging James as though her life depended on it. He was in a pretty bad way and I wasn't sure who was comforting who. I'd grabbed a blanket from the car boot and covered the body with it so they didn't have to see their friend in that state, but the damage was done. That image would forever be imprinted in their memories.

It felt like forever before the police finally arrived, and when they did their insistence that Harry had probably lost control of his bike and caused the accident himself infuriated me. They didn't know what I knew. They didn't know Robert. I had no doubt that he would stoop to murder to accomplish his goal. To me it was obvious that a second vehicle had been involved, and it took some persuading, but eventually they agreed. The evidence was there in front of them, the damage to the rear of the bike, the headlamp glass at the edge of the verge that didn't match the glass on the bike. A forensic team had been called and the road closed off so they could investigate properly. The narrow minded constable who'd arrived first on the scene almost got slapped by Rebel when he continued to blame Harry, insisting the biker must have been responsible and the vehicle that ran into him the victim. Luckily his sergeant put him right before Rebel could raise her arm.

Rebel refused to leave until the coroner arrived and Harry's body was finally removed from the ditch and placed in his van. James was white as a sheet and they both reluctantly agreed to return to the clubhouse.

"We haven't told them," Rebel mumbles quietly as I help her into the passenger seat. She's in no condition to drive and doesn't even notice as I take the keys from her hand where she's been clenching them since she got out of the car earlier.

"It's okay, I'll do it," I offer as I fasten the seatbelt for James. He appears numb, as though he's retreated in on himself.

Today had started off so well, there'd been a lot of laughter, some great banter and everyone was happy. Then Robert had broken in with his twisted reality and destroyed the people that I cared about. As soon as I can I'm going to go and have it out with him. This is too much, it's too extreme and it's sure as hell too high a price to pay for a bloody plot of land.

The drive back to the clubhouse is silent aside from the quiet sobs Rebel has been unable to hold back. When I can, I drive with one hand on the wheel and one hand on her leg, hoping she knows that I am here for her. The gate of the clubhouse opens as soon as the car approaches and I draw in a deep breath, knowing that it's going to be my job to break the bad news to the people inside.

Jackson is in the main room when we enter and one look at Rebel has him running towards her to see what's wrong. The others in the room gather round silently, knowing that whatever it is won't be good news. As soon as she is safe in Jackson's arms Rebel gives way to her grief and almost collapses into him. As he comforts her he looks directly at me for answers. James is sheet white and shaking, it's obvious he's not going to be able to tell them anything.

"We went looking for Harry…" I start. There are times when you just know that bad news is coming. That's the mood in the room right now. It's as though they're all imperceptibly bracing themselves for it. "I'm sorry, there was an accident, it looks like he'd been run off the road. I…" I'm struggling to be the bearer of this awful news.

"Is he dead?" Jackson asks, looking me in the face as he continues to comfort Rebel in his arms.

I can't bring myself to say the words so I just nod. There are a few gasps of horror from the women in the room which quickly turn to sobs.

"But I called him a lazy fekker," Daisy sobs loudly and is quickly drawn into Fingers' embrace.

There's a combination of stunned silence and sobbing throughout the room. It's like everyone's in a limbo and just doesn't know how to react to the news. I'm reluctant to leave Rebel just yet, but desperate for a confrontation with Robert. I can't let these people know that I'm involved in this situation in any way, they'd never forgive me and I'd certainly lose Rebel. I can't let that happen, she means too much to me. I decide that the best thing to do is stay. Robert will wait, for now. It's not as though any decision I make now will bring Harry back.

JACKSON PROMISED to take care of Rebel for me. She'd finally fallen asleep, exhausted from her grief and I'd carried her to her room, laying her on her bed and covering her with a blanket to keep her warm. It's not a cold day, but the shock had left her feeling ice cold all afternoon. He accepted my explanation that I had some work stuff to sort out that couldn't wait, and understood. Life has to go on when someone dies. As much as we want it to just stop and let us grieve, it doesn't. We have to carry on.

Bandit gave me a lift back to Rebel's so I could pick up my truck. The whole drive over to Robert's I tried to hold in my anger. My mother taught me that hate is a strong word and that we shouldn't hate anyone. Surprisingly, she didn't hate Robert for the way that he'd destroyed her life.

She's a strong woman, but on this topic I think she's wrong. I hate Robert with a vengeance. I've never met anyone as despicable and twisted as he is, someone who takes so much pleasure from others misery. I have to rein it in. Roberts feeds off dark emotions, and I refuse to fuel his twisted psyche.

I sit outside in my truck, trying to calm myself down. Thinking of Rebel doesn't help, remembering the grief on her face just fuels the anger. Instead, I try and think of my mother before she got sick. The way her face would light up with love when I entered the room. The soothing words she'd utter when my teenage anger at the father who'd discarded me ran wild and my temper threatened to erupt into violence.

Entering the house I see Deidre scurrying up the stairs, holding her ribs as though she's in pain. She's not a bad woman, I know that. I just don't understand why she stays with him. I knock on the office door and am granted entry. Walking into the room I stand in front of his desk. "Tell me you're not responsible for that young man's death?" I ask him.

"What young man?" He isn't even paying me attention, he's busy on his laptop.

"That young biker you had run off the road," I state.

"He's dead?" Robert genuinely sounds as though he didn't know. "So what, as long as it encourages her to sign that fucking paperwork it doesn't matter." He finally turns his head from the laptop to look at me.

I desperately want to stride over to the desk and pull him up by his throat, but I don't. It takes all the self-restraint that I have. "She won't sign, surely you've realized that by now."

"Oh, she'll sign alright." His quite confidence infuriates me. "She'll sign or she'll lose more people she cares about. It's pretty simple really."

The man is a monster. There will be no reasoning with him. I leave the room as quietly as I entered. I have no idea who he'll target next. Perhaps this has gone on too long and now is the time for me to go to Jackson and come clean. I can't. Whilst my mother relies on his goodwill to keep paying her medical bills I am trapped. I have a horrible feeling that things are about to get a whole lot worse.

CHAPTER THIRTY-SIX

Rebel

Chris has been called away, I woke to a text telling me that his mother had deteriorated in the night and the nursing home had called him in. He'd wanted to stay with me last night, but I'd needed to be alone. I wish now I'd let him stay so I could be there for him today. I know how much his mother means to him, and my heart hurts for him. So much grief fills my heart, for Chris and for Harry and I feel like my limbs weigh a ton. I'm not sure I can drag myself from my bed. Yesterday was horrific and I try to stop the memories from invading my head, but fail. I can't escape the image of Harry's broken body just left there in the ditch, the dried blood on his clothes and the unnatural angle of his head.

My sleep had been dreamless because Chris had insisted I took a sleeping pill before he left. If he couldn't stay with me then he wanted to know that at least I'd get some sleep. The pill has left me feeling lethargic and drowsy, not quite with it. The shower does little to bring me from this hungover state, and I have a sudden yearning not to be on my own. Grabbing my phone I call Jackson and ask him if he'll come over.

"Where's Chris, I thought he was staying with you last night?" Jackson doesn't sound happy.

"I insisted he went home, I just needed to be on my own last night," I confess. "He sent me a text this morning, his mother's taken a turn for the worse so he's been called into the nursing home." Jackson accepts my explanation and agrees to come over. I dress quickly and without conscious thought about what I'm wearing. Glancing in the mirror I catch sight of my reflection and I'm wearing jeans and a sweater. I feel so cold, it's like it's deep within my bones and no matter what I do I can't seem to get warm. The coffee mug in my hands is helping a little. I've foregone breakfast, there's a sick feeling in the pit of my stomach and I'm pretty sure if I tried to eat anything I'd throw up right now. Jackson hasn't arrived yet and I feel the need for comfort so I head to the sofa and curl up, feet underneath me and hugging Rebel Lion to me. Unconsciously I thread the soft fur of his mane through my fingers, there's something comforting about the action. The soft toy makes me feel closer to Chris and I feel sad that I'm not there for him when he needs me in the way that he was there for me yesterday. I'd been a little surprised to wake up at the clubhouse in my room, but Chris was there on the bed beside me and held me when I burst into a round of fresh tears.

We'd stayed there until late, everyone together in the main room sharing memories of Harry.

He was so young, how could his life be snuffed out at twenty two? I hold back a sniffle at the thought that I'll never see him in one his tacky tracksuits again, never call him 'Triple B' and see his face light up with pride at the nickname he never realized was actually an insult. There will be no more 'Billy Big Bollocks'. That makes me so sad, and I grip my lion harder, burying my face in his soft head as the tears start to flow.

I'm grateful when I hear the sound of Jackson pulling up in my car. Chris had insisted I leave it at the clubhouse last night and had brought me home in his truck. I'm still not sure how his truck got from here to there or when, but it's not worth worrying about. I'm just so glad that Jackson is here.

Chastity

I look at the pile of clothes on the bed and can't seem to decide what to pack. It's only for a few days so I can go support Rebel, but I'm still so shocked by the news of Harry's death that I can't seem to concentrate on the task at hand. It doesn't feel two minutes ago that we were all together at the clubhouse, and now I'm returning under such sad circumstances. I try and pull myself together and pull out some jeans and tops, then remember that I haven't got underwear from the drawer yet. Shoes. I need shoes as well and possibly a sweater and a jacket. I try and focus on the packing and not think about what's happened.

I groan when I hear the knock on the door, I can't be doing with cold callers today of all days. I've too much to do to be bothered with them and whatever they're selling, I'm not buying. Perhaps, if I ignore them they'll go away. I stand quietly for a moment but it doesn't work. The knocking repeats but this time it's more insistent and accompanied by a voice shouting my name. What the hell?

Rushing to the door I open it wide and am surprised to see George standing there. "What on earth are you doing here, George? I'm sorry, I'm really busy, I've got to go see Rebel," I politely inform him. I can't say that I'm pleased to see him, there's something slightly off about George, and in my sober state I'm not overly keen on spending any time with him.

"I'm sorry, I was the closest so they asked me to come get you. Rebel needs you," he rushes out.

"I know she needs me, I'm just packing and heading over there already," I assure him. "No need for you to bother, I have it all in hand."

"You don't understand," he protests. "There's been an accident."

"I know there's been an accident." I cut him off. "Harry's dead and I'm heading over to Rebel's as soon as I've finished packing."

His next words stop me dead in my tracks. "No, you don't

understand, it's Rebel, she's been in a crash," he rushes out. "She's in a pretty bad way and Jackson sent me to get you. I've to take you to the hospital."

I'm numb. This can't be happening. First Harry, now Rebel. What the hell is going on? "I, I'll just grab my purse," I manage to stutter out. Shock is slowing my movements and for a moment I can't remember where I left my bag. Spotting it under the coffee table I grab it and rush out of the door, locking it behind me. George motions for me to follow him to his truck. I'm surprised to see two guys in the back, I wasn't expecting that. George obviously notices my concern and assures me that they're just work colleagues, he was on his way to a job when the call came through and they insisted that they were fine with the detour to pick me up and take me to the hospital.

He helps me step up in to the front seat of the truck. The two guys in the back merely nod in greeting. They're creepy looking as hell, but right now I need to concentrate on Rebel. No sooner have I fastened my seatbelt than I feel my head yanked back in my seat, and a large hand covers my mouth before I can scream. I look at George from the corner of my eye and am surprised to see him grinning at me. What the fuck? The hand covering my mouth feels strange and I realize it's a cloth that's covering my mouth, accompanied by a strange odor. Before I can express my anger my eyes become heavy and everything goes black.

CHAPTER THIRTY-SEVEN

Jackson

T he knock at the door is unexpected, judging by the look on Rebel's face. For some reason my gut tells me that I need to remain out of sight. That inner sense has saved me on several occasions over the years and it's blaring alarms at me now. I catch hold of Rebel's arm as she starts to rise from the sofa.

"It's too early for Chastity to be here," she tells me, her face showing her confusion.

"Don't ask why, but I've got a feeling this isn't good news. Answer the door as normal, but don't let on that I'm here. I'll keep out of sight in your room until I know what's going on," I tell her.

Rebel looks at me incredulously, but she trusts me and more importantly, she trusts my instinct. Nodding her agreement she waits until I'm out of the room before heading to the door.

"Oh, hi George. What are you doing here?" She greets the caller. Who the fuck is George?

"I'm here on business if that's okay, do you have a moment?" I don't recognize the voice. He sounds cordial enough but I'm still on high alert.

"Yeah, sure, come on in. Do you want a coffee?" I hear the creak as the door opens wider. I really must remember to bring some oil with me next time I visit, I've been promising to fix that for months for her.

"No, thanks. I don't have a lot of time."

I can hear movement and looking through the crack in the door I see them both move to the sofa and sit down. The guy looks a little embarrassed for some reason, and he can't bring himself to look Rebel in the eye as he talks.

"My boss has asked me to come around and see if you've signed the papers yet," he offers.

"What papers? I'm not sure what you're talking about George. Who is your boss?" Rebel looks and sounds confused.

"The land sale," George replies, still unable to look her in the eye.

"I've no idea what you're talking about, George. I'm not selling any land so there are no papers to sign."

"Oh," he starts. "I'd hoped it wouldn't come to this." He gulps in a breath, clearly nervous and uncomfortable.

"Come to what, George?" Rebel asks him.

"I'm sorry, Rebel. I like you, but my boss isn't a good man. Once he makes his mind up, well, let's just say when he wants something, he gets it." George's voice is full of apology. "I need to show you something." George pulls his phone from his pocket and turns it towards Rebel to show her the screen. I can't see it from here but I can see the look of horror on her face. I realize it's a video when he touches the screen and I can hear faint words, I can't make them out but can clearly see Rebel go white.

"What the fuck?! What are you doing to Chastity!" She screams out. That's enough for me and I shoot into the room, scaring the crap out of George in the process. He shoots up from the sofa, dropping the phone.

"What! Who?" Before he can say anymore I have him pinned back on the sofa, my face menacingly in front of his.

"I don't know who you are or who you work for, but you're messing with the wrong family. What the fuck is going on?" I demand, my breath hot against his face. He's a well-built guy but he's no match for me, and from his reaction his heart was never in this role he's been asked to perform.

"I, I, I..." He's so surprised right now he can't get his

words out. It doesn't take long though for a mask to fall across his face and his bravado to return.

"Fuck you!" He snarls at me. "I'm not telling you shit." I lash out, my fist connecting with his jaw and temporarily stunning him. Pulling my gun on him to keep him quiet, I turn to Rebel for an explanation. She's crying quietly, but reaches down to pick up the phone so she can show me the video. When she hits play I see Chastity tied to a chair in a dark room. She has a black eye and a fat lip but looks straight into the camera, anger radiating from her.

"Don't do jack shit these tossers ask of you Rebel," she states. A fist appears from nowhere and punches her. Rebel is crying. Off camera a voice is giving instructions. Either Rebel signs the land sale paperwork she has been sent, or she will have her friend returned to her in pieces. The video cuts off suddenly as Chastity starts cursing again.

Rebel is distraught, as much as I'd like to comfort her I need to concentrate on the piece of shit in front of me. She doesn't need to see this. I know exactly what I need to do.

"Darlin', I need you to get me some rope and some gaffa tape. I'll sort this for you," I promise her. It says something that she doesn't question me, she just heads off to the kitchen to find what I asked for. She returns a moment later holding some cable ties and thick black tape.

"These do?" She shows them to me.

"Perfect," I reply. "Fasten his hands behind his back with the ties and cover his mouth with the tape." I move the gun closer to George's face to encourage him to behave whilst Rebel incapacitates him.

"What about his feet?" She looks at me for instruction, calm as a cucumber.

"Nah, wait till he's in the car before we do that."

"Where are you taking him?" She's curious, but not concerned.

"No need to bother yourself with that, you stay here. Try not to panic. I'll bring Chastity back as soon as I can," I promise her. George rolls his eyes at my confidence, but he's underestimated Rebel's family and our shared past. I'm confident I can deliver. I pat him down and find what I'm looking for in his pocket, the keys to his truck. Throwing him over my shoulder we head outside. Rebel lets out a gasp when she sees the truck on her driveway. She moves closer, inspecting it. "This is the truck that James saw," she gasps out. She moves to the front of the vehicle where the damage is obvious, the headlight is smashed and there are dents all over the bumper and scratches on the bonnet. "This is the truck that killed Harry." She's gone as white as a sheet, but doesn't hesitate to help me manhandle him into the vehicle. "Bring her home safe." She begs me.

"I will, I promise," I reassure her, hoping that this isn't a promise I will need to break.

It doesn't take long to get him secured in the back of his truck, and I watch her in the rear view mirror, standing on the doorstep watching me drive off. There's a hesitant wave of her hand before she slowly heads inside and closes the door behind her.

My phone has connected to the vehicles hand's free system so I call the clubhouse and arrange for a couple of the guys to meet me, and bring the supplies that I'll need. It's a simple but effective technique I'm planning to use, and I'm confident it will get George to reveal where they're holding Chastity.

It doesn't take long to reach the old warehouse. The bikes and van outside show me the guys are here and waiting for me.

Bandit walks over to greet me, giving me a one armed hug and Aaron and Ryan are with him.

"What do you need us to do?" Bandit asks.

"Chastity has been kidnapped, the guy in the back knows where she is. Let's get him inside and fastened down and I have just the thing to get him to talk. Did you bring the fuel can?" I don't tell them that Rebel thinks this is the guy who killed Harry, I can't afford to let their anger and need for revenge loose just yet. I'll save that for later.

Bandit grins at me, he loves the fuel can trick. It's never failed yet. "Sure did. This should be fun."

"Fuel can?" Ryan looks confused, he's never seen it done before.

"Just watch and learn, this should be interesting for you," Aaron tells him.

Aaron and Ryan effortlessly lift George from the car boot and carry him inside.

By the time Bandit and I have joined them, George is already secured to a wooden chair, arms tied behind his back and his ankles to the chair legs. I indicate for the guys to stand behind me and they move against the wall, casually leaning against it and waiting for the show to start.

George doesn't look scared, just furious. The tape across his mouth prevents him vocalizing his feelings, but his eyes say it all. Slowly I move towards him and rip the tape from his mouth. It leaves an angry red trace, I know how much that will have stung but he doesn't show it.

"So, George. I need you to tell me where Chastity is, who else is there and what weapons they've got." I stand facing him, just a few paces away from the chair.

"Fuck you!" He snarls in return. It's not like I expected him to volunteer the details. Slowly I reach down for the petrol can beside my feet. I show it to him, the hand holding it moving slightly so he can hear the swish of the fuel inside. I have to give him credit for his bravado, but I've yet to see any man who hasn't broken using this technique. I move towards him, releasing the cap of the fuel can as I do. His eyes track my progress, betraying no alarm until I start to pour the liquid over his head, it flows down his body, soaking his clothes, yet there's enough left to pool at his feet. The fumes permeate the building and are bringing tears to his eyes. Still he looks on impassively.

I accept the box of matches from Bandit who has suddenly appeared at my side, then returns to his place leaning against the wall with the others. The wall that is next to the door, the only exit from the building.

"The only thing flammable in here is you." I shake the box of matches at George.

"Fuck, Uncle Jackson," I hear from behind me. "When you invited me to a barbecue I wasn't expecting this!" Ryan sounds amused, he's enjoying watching this. I know he has a soft spot for Chastity, that's why I let him stay and watch.

I lean menacingly forward, into George's face. "I'll ask you one more time. Where is Chastity, who else is there and what weapons they've got."

He's tough, I'll give him that. He maintains his stone faced silence until I draw a match from the box and strike it against the side. As the flame comes to life he starts to babble the answers I need. To encourage him to be more forthcoming I blow out the match I'm holding. It works and he reveals yet more details. I turn to the guys behind me, checking that they recorded everything we needed.

"Thank you," I smile at him. It's a cold smile. I turn to the guys nodding that it's time for them to leave. Ryan hesitates in the doorway, aware that this isn't the end of what I have planned for George, and watches curiously. I pull another match from the box and light it. "But you shouldn't have messed with my daughter." George's face is a mask of horror as I flick the lit match and it slowly travels down to the pool of fuel at his feet.

"No!" He screams. "I told you everything." He's sobbing now and I can see the tell-tale signs that he's lost control of his bladder. I turn my back on his screams and head for the door.

"What the fuck?" Ryan laughs as I reach him.

The match lands on the floor and sizzles out as it hits the water there. That's right, swapping the fuel for water is an old trick, but effective and hasn't failed me yet. I leave the building, shutting the door behind me and ignoring George's angry screams. Ryan looks at me with interest.

"We'll let him go later, right now we need to go get Chastity."

He nods his head in agreement, he's in this with us as we head back to the vehicles and call in for reinforcements. It's time to go rescue our girl.

CHAPTER THIRTY-EIGHT

Jackson

I've phoned the clubhouse and a couple more of the guys are heading out to join us, bringing some more weapons with them. I know the location of the old house where she's being held. It's pretty remote so that plays in our favor in one respect, there'll be no one to overhear us, although it will make access harder. We've arranged to meet everyone at the crossroads on the main road. When we get there they've arrived ahead of us, they're a welcome sight.

No one bothers asking why we're doing this, it's good enough for them that I asked for help. I briefly fill them in and let them know it's Chastity in there and we need to get her out. As soon as they hear her name their shoulders stiffen. She's one of us, part of our family.

"I assume this means we leave no one behind?" Fingers asks.

"That's right," I confirm. "They're doing this to get to Rebel, and they're not going to get away with hurting either of our girls." There's a chorus of approval from the assembled men.

I open the map of the area on the bonnet of the car and we work out where each of us will enter from so that we can cover all the exits. Ryan is happy to play the role of decoy in case they recognize any of us. The story is that he's come off his bike and got lost looking for help. He reluctantly rolls around on the gravel road covering his leather jacket and jeans in dust and even goes as far as scratching the gravel along his cheek. When he stands back up he looks the part.

It's a fifteen minute walk on foot from the main road, but we make good time, slowing down the closer we get to minimize any sign or sound from our approach.

When we hit the tree line at the front of the property we split off, all heading in our assigned directions. I hope that the intel George gave us was right, and that Chastity is safe, or he'll be on the receiving end of my anger when we return.

The house sits before us, broken and silent against the arid landscape. It's not been empty for many years, but nature has been quick to act. Storms have loosened the shutters which now hang askew on the windows and something has been eating away at the porch. We'll need to watch our step as it's looking a touch rotten underfoot.

It's a simple design with two windows separated by a front door on the ground floor, and two windows above. Aaron and I stay out of sight behind the lone vehicle parked in front and watch as Ryan approaches the door, dragging his ankle in the dust in case anyone is watching.

His knock isn't as strong as it could be, but he is trying to give the impression he's hurt and needs assistance. There's no answer to the first couple of knocks so Ryan adds a convincing pained plea for help.

"Please, I know you're in there, I can see the car. I came off my bike and I think I've broken my ankle. I need help." Ryan continues to bang at the front door. He cocks his head, listening, and obviously satisfied that someone is coming to answer he gives the signal for us to be ready.

The guy who answers the door looks reluctant to let Ryan in, as we expected. Ryan imperceptibly inches closer as he continues to plead for assistance, until he's effectively blocking the door from shutting.

There's a muffled conversation between someone deeper in the house and the guy who answered the door. He's obviously been told not to let Ryan in and tries to shut the door on him. He looks confused when the door won't shut, and then alarmed when Ryan stops slouching and stands at his full height.

Silently Ryan holds a knife to the guys throat, whispering

instructions in the man's ear. That's the cue for Aaron and I to head on up and enter the house. As we pass Ryan he whispers in the guy's ear again, I catch the word 'family', then watch as the knife slices across his throat. Ryan holds him the whole time, almost hugging him, then gently lowers the body to the floor, leaving a clear access to the door. He indicates for us to continue with a nod of his head, turning back to keep an eye on the entrance.

Even though George was adamant there were only two men holding Chastity, we still proceed with caution. I'm certain he told us everything, but better safe than sorry. The furniture is still in the house, covered in grimy dust sheets, weird outlines that can't be identified. From the dust on the floor it looks like the lounge hasn't been disturbed, the footprints and scuffs show a trail to the rear of the house. The door to what we think is the dining room is closed. Cautiously I turn the handle, hoping the hinges are oiled. Again the dust inside indicates this room hasn't been disturbed in quite some time.

There's noise coming from the back of the house, the kitchen spans the whole rear and should have a small pantry and utility on the far right. The door is ajar and Aaron has his eye to the crack. Stealthily he moves back to me and signs that there's one perpetrator in there to the left. Chastity is in there and close to him. We need to be careful now, if we surprise him and he's armed he may try and use her as a shield. The element of surprise is on our side and we plan on using it.

Aaron moves back to the door and when he's happy I'm at his back kicks it open.

"What the fuck? Who are you?" The guy is an amateur, he's frozen in shock at the sight of Aaron standing in front of him, a gun aimed at his head. "Take her, she's not worth dying for."

Aaron orders him to release Chastity from the ropes that bind her to the chair. As soon as she's released Chastity runs over to me, her face a mess of tears. I hold her close, and gently remove the gag from her mouth. She sags into my arms and starts bawling. I pick her up and cradle her, whispering soothing words of comfort to her, telling her she's going to be okay. She's safe now. Her head moves a little to the side and she's starting at the guy who still has Aaron's gun pointed at him. Her face is a mask of fear.

Aaron moves a step closer to the guy who visibly pales the closer he gets. Taking the barrel of his gun he teases it down the guys cheek, shaking his head as he does so.

"You were wrong," he waves the gun in his face. "She is worth dying for." With that Aaron pulls the trigger. Chastity flinches in my arms as the sound fills the kitchen and the body slumps to the floor, one neat head shot ending his life.

Aaron opens the back door and shouts to let the others know it's done. Fingers is going back for one of the vehicles as Chastity is in shock and far too unsteady to make the trek back.

Ryan steps into the kitchen and surveys the body on the floor. "Nice shot. You want me to get a clean-up crew in?" He offers.

"A clean-up crew? How the hell do you have access to one of those?" I ask, my voice full of shock. "On second thoughts I don't want to know." I look to Aaron to see what he wants to do, he's the president after all.

"Nah, leave em. Let them know what they're up against." He shrugs. "They need to know that they can't mess with our family."

CHAPTER THIRTY-NINE

Rebel

R elief flows through me as I pack an overnight bag, they've found Chastity and she's going to be okay. They're taking her back to the clubhouse as she refused to go to the hospital to be checked out which sounds exactly like my stubborn friend. Jackson wants me to head over there, not just because he knows I need to go and see for myself that my friend's okay, but he's concerned about my safety after the revelation that George's truck was the one that killed Harry. He didn't say it but I know we have to talk. I'm not sure how or even why, but all the events of the past few days seem to be connected to the land sale agreement that I'm being pestered to sign. It just doesn't make sense that someone would go to such extraordinary lengths for a bit of land.

I smile as my phone starts ringing and I can see it's my

mom on the other end. I wonder what's wrong as it's not that long since she left. I'd called her when Jackson left as I hated being left here on my own, not knowing what was happening. She'd rushed over and sat with me, only leaving when Jackson called to say they had Chastity and she was safe.

"Hi, mom, what's up?" I greet her.

"Rebel, I don't have long. I can't explain it all now but you've got to get out of there." There's a panicked tone to her voice that has me worried.

"What do you mean?"

"They're coming for you, I'm sorry. I tried to protect you but Robert found out they found Chastity and he's sent them after you. He's furious. You've got to get out of there now!" She's started sobbing now.

"I don't understand!" What on earth is she talking about? I can hear something in the background but it's muffled and I can't make it out properly. "Is this to do with our conversation earlier?"

"Yes, I told him what you said about never selling the land and he's gone ballistic. He's never hurt me that much before. You've got to get out of there, I'm scared for you, I really think they're going to kill you."

What the hell? I can't believe anyone in their right mind would react like that to being told no. I know mom hasn't had it easy living with Robert but he's not a murderer surely. I can't grasp that I could be in danger just because I said no.

"Of course they won't kill me, you're worrying about nothing," I try to reassure her.

"You don't understand, you don't know what he's capable of. You've got to get out of there now!" Her tone is firm, but she's not shouting at me. There's a banging noise in the background of the call, it sounds like someone is hammering loudly on a door. That could be the muffled noise, someone shouting to be let in.

"What's happening there?" I ask, I'm starting to panic now, not for myself but for mom. Whatever is happening on the other end of the phone does not sound good.

"He's trying to get in, I think he's realized I'm trying to warn you. Please, Rebel," she sobs out, "please get out of there now. Go somewhere safe. Go to Jackson, he'll protect you. I can't lose you now I've found you." She's crying heavily now. I still can't believe what she's saying but decide to humor her anyway. I keep the phone to my ear as I grab my bag and car keys.

"Okay, I'm heading out now. I'll go to Jackson but I'm sure you're worrying about nothing," I reassure her.

"Run, you've got to get out of there now!!!" Mom screams at the other end of the phone at the same time I hear a huge crash.

"Mom!" I shout down the phone but she's not answering. I

think she's dropped her phone as everything sounds different. I can hear a man's voice shouting and mom crying.

"You stupid bitch!" The man's voice is louder now. "You had one job to do and you couldn't even do that," he snarls. There's a dull noise that I can't place but each time I hear it mom moans in pain. Is the bastard hitting her?

I've been so shocked at what's happening that I've been quiet, but now I scream her name into the phone.

"What the fuck?" The thudding noise stops as the man shouts. "You rang her? You're even more stupid than I thought."

I've never heard so much venom in a voice before. I need to help her, but I don't know what to do. I've got my car unlocked and dock my phone, switching it to hands free so I can concentrate on driving away from here as quickly as possible. I'm tempted to drive to her, but I know that deep down I'm going to be no match for whoever is in there with her. I just have to get to Jackson, he'll know what to do.

I can hear my mom pleading with the man, begging him not to hurt me. Tears start falling down my face, I feel so helpless. I need to be there. I need to do something. I need to ring Jackson, let him know what's happening but I can't hang up, I need to keep the connection open for her, to let her know that help is coming.

"Help's coming mom," I shout into the phone, regretting the words as soon as I hear the response from the other end. There's a shuffling sound then the man's voice comes down the phone clearly, he's obviously picked it up.

"Too late." The man lets out a maniacal laugh and I can hear my mother begging in the background.

"No!" She screams out. "I love you, Rebel, never forget that!"

The explosion of noise from the phone startles me, I almost drift over into the other lane of the highway. I can't hear anything from mom and I'm scared.

"You're next." The voice comes through the phone, the cold tone sending shivers through me. The line is cut off and fear fills me. That noise was a gun going off. I'm sure of it. Panic causes my fingers to fumble as I try and reach Jackson, I can't hit the speed dial. I'm shaking too much.

The road around me is deserted but I can see a cloud of dust moving towards the back of my car at speed. It could just be someone driving too fast, but considering the call I just had I'd be stupid to believe that. I suspect it's whoever mom said was coming for me. I put the pedal to the floor, praying that I have enough of a lead to get away from them. I don't understand what's happening. This is like something out of a movie, a crazy messed up movie at that.

I finally manage to hit the button for Jackson's phone but it just rings out. Please answer the phone, I scream at my mobile. I know that he can't hear me, but I'm scared. His voicemail clicks in and I hang up and redial. He's got to answer. My chest is burning from heartache and my hands are shaking so badly I can barely connect with the phone screen. It's a twenty minute drive from my house to the clubhouse on a normal day, but today I'm pushing my car to its limits and beyond grateful that most of the route is straight. Every minute feels like it lasts forever. There's still no answer from Jackson's phone but I keep hanging up and redialing regardless. I can't seem to take a full breath and gasp in oxygen in short bursts. The car in the rear mirror is gaining on me, but there's still a distance between us. I can only pray that it's enough of a gap to get me to the clubhouse in time. I can barely see the road in front of me for the tears that are falling. Instinct is keeping me on the road, I've driven this route so many times it's ingrained. It's all so surreal that it feels like I'm watching from the outside in, this can't really be happening to me. My head is pounding from all the crying, and I'm more scared than I've ever been in my life.

I have a sudden thought and hit the speed dial for my mom's phone instead, desperate for her to answer. Instead of ringing it gives me a solid tone. Has he destroyed her phone? Please let her be okay, I pray loudly as I continue to push my car to its limits. I try Jackson again, one last time and this time he answers.

"Sorry, darlin'" he answers gently, and before he can continue with his explanation I interrupt.

"He killed her, he killed mom." I sob down the phone. "He's going to kill me…"

"What the hell?" Jackson yells. "What's happening? Where are you?"

I look around me trying to work out where I am on the route, I'm minutes away now but the car in the mirror is gaining on me.

"I'm almost at the clubhouse but they're chasing me," I sob. "They're going to kill me."

I can hear Jackson shouting orders in the background, he's getting them to open the gate for me and making sure that they've got their weapons at hand just in case.

"Rebel, I need you to try and calm down darlin', concentrate on the road." His voice is soothing, calming. It's no good, I'm still hysterical although some survival instinct must be at work as I haven't crashed the car yet. Rounding the corner I finally see the clubhouse, not slowing down as I approach the gate, just hoping it will be open by the time I reach it. I hit the brakes as I fly through the gate and that's when I lose control of the car, I broke too hard and the car isn't responding to the steering wheel. It's heading for the clubhouse. I've no idea how I get it back under control, but somehow I do. Ingrained training kicks in and I wrestle the car to a stop just short of a collision. The car has barely come to a standstill before my door is yanked open and Jackson is there. I can't undo my seatbelt, I'm almost hyperventilating by now. He reaches over and releases me, helping me from the car and drawing me into his arms.

"He killed her," I sob loudly. "He killed my mom."

CHAPTER FORTY

Chris

The front door is wide open and I have a horrible feeling that I am too late. Robert went ballistic when he heard that Chastity had escaped. He thinks that Deidre turned on him. I tried to tell him it wasn't possible, she didn't even know he'd taken Chastity, never mind where she was being held. I'd refused to have any part of it. Aside from my moral objections, the call from the nursing home had put paid to any loyalty I had left to him.

The call came in at three am, a pleasant but apologetic nurse interrupting my sleep to give me the news that my mother was unlikely to make it through the night and requesting my presence. I knew it was coming, but it was like a punch to the gut hearing the words. I've never moved as quickly, dragging on yesterday's clothes and running for my car. Thanks to the late hour the roads were clear and I managed to get there in record time, although I suspect a speeding offense might land on my doormat in the near future. It's a small price to pay for being able to share those last few moments with her.

She's not really known who I am for months now. Cancer had eaten away at her body, and her mind until she could no longer care for herself. That's why I had to work for Robert and keep him sweet, I couldn't afford the nursing home fees. I figured it was the least he could do for her, having ignored her all my life. He'd have refused, selfish to the end that man, if I hadn't suggested I have a chat with a journalist friend of mine about my parentage and upbringing. It had come at a price, he insisted I work for him so he could keep tabs on me, not to mention constantly remind me what was at stake for me if I failed to comply.

The room was peaceful and tranquil when I got there. A nurse had been sitting with her so she wasn't alone, but she gratefully relinquished her seat for me and returned to her shift. The staff there have been outstanding, showing genuine care and compassion for the few months' she's been a resident. I knew she was so heavily drugged she'd probably not know I was there, even if she did, I don't think she'd have remembered who I was or what we mean to each other. Still, I sat there holding her hand and telling her stories of the good times we'd shared, of the love I had for her and even telling her about Rebel. They'd have loved each other, it's a shame they never got the chance to meet.

The dawn chorus was just breaking and the first rays of dawn were appearing through the cracks in the curtain when she passed. She's finally at peace now. No more suffering. And in her way, she's released me from my debt to my father. I just hope it's not too late to save Deidre.

I can hear shouting from the study and pray that I'm in time. Before I can get to the door there's a scream followed by a loud shot that echoes through the house. Fuck. I draw my gun and gingerly push the door open, afraid of what I am going to find on the other side. Deidre is collapsed at the side of the desk and there's blood all over her blouse. Robert is standing in front of her, ranting and raving at her, seemingly oblivious that he's shot her. He's waving the gun around in front of him and still telling her that it's all her fault.

"You're a worthless slut," he hisses at her, and moves to kick her already broken body.

"Stop right there," I shout out, startling him. "That's the last time you hurt a woman." I promise him, my gun aimed between his eyes. The look he gives me is feral, he's lost whatever tiny shred of sanity he's been operating on for these last few months. I notice a movement in front of him and decide to let things play out, making it my job to keep him distracted.

I can barely make sense of the insults he's throwing my way, spittle flying from his mouth, but I do hear the words bastard and cocksucker.

Behind him, Deidre has pulled the letter opener from the

desk and is gripping it in her hand. It's a sharp knife, similar to a stiletto. Robert bought it from someone who swore it belonged to one of the original Italian mafia dons. His prized possession is going to cost him a lot more than he ever thought possible.

He mentions my mother in the next breath and it takes everything I have within me not to pull the trigger and blow the hideous excuse of a man away. I don't, because Deidre deserves her moment. I've seen what he's put her through, heard the beatings, seen her limp away to lick her wounds. She gives him a look of pure disgust just before she thrusts the knife blade into him. From her position on the floor she hasn't been able to gain much height, but I think it's poetic justice that the blade pierces his groin. I just hope she's managed to sever an artery and bring an end to his miserable existence. It's too much effort for her though, and she loses her grip of the knife, sinking further down into the floor, her eyes closing. Keeping my gun aimed at Robert, who has now sunk to his knees in shock and pain, I pull my cell from my pocket and call the emergency services, asking for both police and medics. I report a shooting and a stabbing, and advise that the shooting was attempted murder. Only when I'm sure they're on their way do I rush over to Deidre to see if there is anything I can do for her. I ignore Robert who's curled up on himself, keening away in pain with his hands hovering over the blade, unsure whether to pull it out or not. There's enough blood around the entrance wound that I hope he does remove it. I want the bastard to bleed to death, slowly and painfully. I want him to suffer for what he's done to me, my mother, Deidre and Rebel. Who knows how many more lives he has destroyed along the way.

I drop down to Deidre and breathe a sigh of relief when I feel a pulse, albeit a very faint one. "Stay with me, Deidre, helps on the way."

"What about me?" Robert whines beside us, he's attempting to crawl away and make his escape. That can't happen. I stand quickly and without thinking smash my foot down on his ankle, taking too much pleasure from the audible crack I hear. He's crying like a baby and can't decide where to place his hands, on his speared dick or his broken ankle. I don't care. Now I know he's not going anywhere, I turn my attention back to Deidre.

I pull my t-shirt over my head and use it to apply pressure to the wound on her shoulder. If I can reduce the blood loss, I'm hopeful she can make it until the medics arrive. I apply more pressure as the t-shirt soaks through with blood. Deidre's eyes flutter slightly and she opens them just long enough to look up at me.

"Tell Rebel I love her," she whispers, her breath thready and weak.

"Tell her yourself, Deidre, stay with me, she needs you!" I sob, tears falling down my own face. "Deidre!" I scream at her but she's unresponsive.

The sound of sirens get closer and it's not long before bodies fly into the room with us. I'm soon pushed aside so the medics can work on Deidre and Robert. A policeman takes my arm and leads me into the hallway where we're not in the way.

"What happened in there?" he asks me.

"Robert shot his wife, he was trying to kill her. He's lost his mind, although he's been abusing her for years. She managed to grab the letter opener and stabbed him. Is she going to be alright?" I've started shaking so the police officer guides me over to a nearby chair, calling for a blanket. He thinks I'm going into shock. "Is she going to be alright?" I ask again, desperate for news.

He looks behind my shoulder at the scene still playing out in the study, then shakes his head. "It doesn't look good mate, I'm sorry." I close my eyes and let my body be taken over by sobs. I've failed them all, how on earth can I ever face Rebel again?

EPILOGUE

Rebel - One Year Later

It's a gloriously sunny morning, it should be a perfect day for the dedication. Whilst it's going to be an emotional day, I know I'll have the ones I love by my side to support me. Who knew just how much my life would change in just a year. If you'd told me back then how radically different my life would be today, I wouldn't have believed you. I'd have huffed my disbelief, and I'd have been wrong.

"Babe, have we got any more shower gel?" Chris's voice comes through the en-suite door. I wish he'd learn to check before he steps in the shower, but not Chris. I chuckle, easing myself from our comfortable bed, and head into the en-suite to find the shower gel in the cupboard under the sink. It took a little while to adjust to sharing my sanctuary with someone else, but Chris loves our home as much as I do. I thought it would seem much smaller with him here, but instead it feels cozy and homely. He moved in a few months ago when Robert's house sold, it felt like the most natural thing in the world and still does. It was a bit of a contrast for him as he'd been living in a basic room in the servant's quarters at Robert's. When he'd asked me if I'd go apartment hunting with him, I suggested he move in with me instead. The timing felt right to me, and we're pretty solid as a couple now. If anything, it brought us closer.

The aftermath of the shooting and Chastity's kidnapping hit the media big time and my name was all over it. I couldn't turn on the local news or pick up a newspaper without seeing my face staring back at me. It was a horrible time to live through. Robert survived his stabbing, although he was a lesser man for it. Despite the amount of evidence incriminating him, he insisted he was innocent. It didn't do him any good and he ended up in prison awaiting trial. The thought of reliving it all again scared the hell out of me. I needn't have worried. Having failed to deliver on the debt he owed, Robert's partners took justice into their own hands and he was shanked in a prison fight. I feel like I should have some kind of sympathy for him, but I don't. He was a horrible, brutal man who destroyed the lives of everyone around him. I will never forgive him for what he did to my mom, when we'd only just discovered each other.

I'm so distracted by my thoughts that I'm not paying attention. Instead of Chris reaching out of the door for the shower gel he pulls me in with him. I gasp as the warm water drenches me. "Chris!" I protest. "I'm getting wet."

Chris chuckles and pulls me closer, so our wet flesh is touching. "I love it when you're wet for me." The look he gives me is so full of love and adoration, I melt. I can't believe that this guy chose me. I throw my arms around his neck and return the kiss he gives me. The shower is so full of heat, and it's not from the water. Forgetting everything else I need to do, I give in and enjoy some one on one time with my man instead.

"REBEL CALM DOWN. You'll be fine," Jackson reassures me. I'm starting to panic. Pulling aside the blind on the window I can see the sea of faces outside, in front of the make shift stage that has been set up for the ceremony. There are familiar faces like Bandit and Smokey, Aaron and Cilla, Fingers and Daisy, and Ryan is out there with Chastity. He's even brought his friends with him. Declan, Holly, Cam and Sahara are such great people and they fit right into our family. They're all dressed up for the occasion in suits and smart dresses, even Jackson is wearing a suit for my special day.

Jackson comes over and hands me a glass. "Chris said I should give you this," he tells me with a smirk on his face. I look at the contents of the glass, it's a shot of Fireball. Chris knows me so well. I accept the glass and sip it slowly.

"Am I doing the right thing?" I ask Jackson.

"Without a doubt," he reassures me. "I couldn't be prouder of you, darlin', you're doing an amazing thing." Jackson has been beside me every step of the way since I made my decision. I know it's the right thing to do, but it's such a huge step and I want to make sure I do it right. Jackson gestures to the sea of faces outside the window. "They're all here for you, darlin', they support you and love you. Now let's get this show on the road. This is your day, and you deserve to enjoy it."

I smooth down the non-existent creases in my tailored suit and adjust the collar on the smart white blouse before taking in a deep breath. Letting it out slowly I nod to Jackson. I'm ready. He reaches for my arm and escorts me through the open front door to the stage outside.

Once on the dais behind the microphone I take a moment to appreciate what is happening. Everyone seated in front of me, including a host of reporters, is here to celebrate what we've achieved. This is a special day.

"I'd like to begin by thanking you all for coming. As you know, today is about celebrating what we've built and looking forward to a brighter future, but for me it's also about remembering my past and being grateful for the opportunities and love that I have received. As a child I never knew my mother, for her own reasons she felt it was safer for me to not be a part of her life. She made a sacrifice I can't begin to comprehend, and despite not having a mother's love growing up, I never wanted for anything. I was brought up by my amazing dads'," I pause a moment to move my arms to indicate Jackson behind me and my dads' from the front row. "Not every child is fortunate enough to have that. Some of my best memories growing up are the times we spent here on this land just camping out, fishing, sharing stories under the stars and being free. Those memories are one of the main reasons I could never see this land developed into some huge commercial concrete structure, and in the aftermath of the horrific events last year, I realized what I needed to do. I wanted to give children without families the opportunity to make those memories of their own, and I wanted to give them a safe place to do that." I turn to indicate the house behind me. I suppose calling it a house is a slight understatement, it's a huge wooden ranch house big enough to accommodate twenty kids at a time along with their carers. There are bunk houses, stables, and out buildings to go with it. "I couldn't have done this alone. This place was built by the local community, it's being run by volunteers, and is funded by generous donations. This is our way of giving back, of showing our love and support to those who don't have families to support them, to love them, to cherish them and care for them." There's an impromptu round of applause that interrupts my words. I hope I'm doing this speech justice. No matter how many times I've read it back, it still doesn't feel enough.

I pick up the extra-large scissors from the rostrum and wave them in the air before me. "I think that's enough waffling from me! I'm sure you guys are ready to toast this place with a glass of champagne!" There's a chorus of cheers from the audience.

I step to the center of the stage, in front of the ribbon that announces the official opening of the 'Double D' ranch.

"I'd like to invite the person who made all this possible to cut the ribbon. I turn and hand the scissors to the woman standing beside me. "This ranch is named in her honor, without her tireless work and endless fundraising and organization this place wouldn't be here. Please welcome DeeDee Delaney, my mom." I place a kiss on her cheek and step back, into the warm embrace of Chris's arms.

There was a time, after that phone call, when I never thought I'd see my mom again. I thought she was dead. It was touch and go for a while, I know the medics thought they'd lost her at the house, but she's a fighter. She pulled through and surprised them all. Our relationship has gone from strength to strength. I love the woman she has become since she was freed from the life Robert had her imprisoned in. She's still having counseling, but each day she gets stronger, becomes more her own woman. As soon as she could, she sold the house they'd shared and donated all the proceeds to the Double D foundation to help build this place. She lives at the clubhouse now, she was welcomed with open arms, and it makes me so happy that all my family are together there. She wears a constant smile on her face these days and is the most loving and giving person you could ever hope to meet. I am so proud to be her daughter.

"Thank you everyone for being here today," she greets the crowd. "Rebel?" She calls me over. "This is a part of both of us, we should do this together." Placing my hand on hers she cuts the ribbon, it flutters to the ground either side of us.

"I declare the 'Double D ranch open!" She shouts, "Now let's go get drunk." Laughter fills the air and we're surrounded by warm greetings, hugs and kisses. There are pats on the back from the attending media, and their promise of future support.

So much has changed in the course of a year, but looking around me at what we have built, both in materials and relationships, I couldn't ask for anything more.

We've built love, hope and a promise of a brighter future.

We've built family.

ACKNOWLEDGMENTS

This book didn't follow the story I had in my head. I lost count of the number of times the words on the page told a different story to the one that I had intended. Heather Woodman was there every painful step of the way, allowing me to bounce ideas off her and feeding my imagination until I was happy with the words on the page. She also played a huge part in keeping the spelling and grammar in check, as did Nikki Costello.

Franessca Wingfield created the amazing cover that gave birth to this story and I cannot thank her enough.

My book besties K L Shandwick and T L Wainwright encouraged me every step of the way and as always verbally kicked me into shape when I was losing the will to write.

The biggest thanks as always has to go to the readers,

without you, there wouldn't be a Rebel. You are the reason I write.

To my crazy number one stalker Margaret Hassebrock and number two stalker Beckie Hughes, you don't know how much it means to have readers who love me like you guys do and meeting you at signings has been an amazing experience.

To Yvonne Eason, Chele McKenzie, Lesley Edwards and Colette Goodchild, who have been there for me through some hard times and sad memories, thank you.

And to everyone else who I should have named and probably forgot, thank you!

#bookfamily

ABOUT THE AUTHOR

AVA MANELLO

Ava is a passionate reader, blogger, publisher, and author

who loves nothing more than helping other Indie authors publish their books be that reviewing, beta reading, formatting or proofreading. She will always be a reader first and foremost.

She loves erotic suspense that's well written and engages the reader, and loves promoting the heck out of it for her favorite authors.

STALK AVA MANELLO

Amazon Author Page
http://geni.us/AvaM

Ava Manello Reader Group (Facebook)
https://www.facebook.com/groups/613212832386624

Ava Manello Facebook Page
http://www.facebook.com/AvaManello

Ava Manello Website
http://www.avamanello.co.uk

Ava Manello Twitter
http://www.twitter.com/AvaManello

Ava Manello Instagram
https://www.instagram.com/avamanello

Ava Manello BookBub

https://www.bookbub.com/authors/ava-manello

Ava Manello Newsletter

http://eepurl.com/bOJXE9

The Non Adventures of Alice the Erotic Author

Amazon: http://geni.us/AliceNonAdventures

Other Channels: https://books2read.com/u/bzPvVq

Severed Angel (Severed MC #1)

Amazon: http://geni.us/SAFREE

Other Channels: https://www.books2read.com/b/bxg5k4

Carnal Desire (Severed MC #2)

Amazon: http://geni.us/CarnalDesire

Other Channels: https://www.books2read.com/b/4j1nDm

Severed Justice(Severed MC #3)

Amazon: http://geni.us/severedjustice

Other Channels: https://www.books2read.com/b/bWrlz4

Carnal Persuasion (Severed MC #4)

Amazon: http://geni.us/CarnalPersuasion

Other Channels: https://www.books2read.com/b/baBG23

31128606R00157

Printed in Poland
by Amazon Fulfillment
Poland Sp. z o.o., Wrocław